WITHIN THE HOLLOW HEART

MELISSA WRIGHT

Cover design and illustration by Ireen Chau

Interior illustrations by

Ireen Chau https://www.ireenchau.com

Silversteampunk @silversteampunk

Grace Crandall @krasnetigritsa

WITHIN

THE

HOLLOW HEART

Nickolas Brigham was going to marry a princess. She would be beautiful and charming and hang on his every word. She would be flawless. Incomparable. Her station would be high enough to place him securely in the ranks of Westrende's most prominent citizens. A princess was indeed the answer to all his problems, and he would marry her posthaste. He just needed to find her first.

"What is the highest rank in the kingdom again?"

His mother glared at him over the rim of her teacup.

"Oh, that's right. I'd forgotten. There is no king, only the council ruling in his stead. No king, no princesses. And among council, the youngest, I believe, is aged around two and forty. So..."

"So the highest-ranking match you'll secure is already beneath us." She made a tsk of disapproval. "Honestly, Nickolas, your great-grandfather dined with a king. Your great-aunt was gifted a horse by another. It should not be so difficult to tie yourself to a woman of station, given the esteem of our family name."

Nickolas gave her a look. She placed her cup on a finely carved side table and glared into the distance as if she'd not noticed his response. Nickolas moved to stare in the same direction, crossing his arms in his finely tailored suit and finding nothing but a finely papered section of wall between a pair of finely painted floral arrangements. He glanced at his mother over a shoulder. Her hair—darker blond than his and just starting to reveal its first strands of silver—was drawn back into a flawless bun, her attire impeccable. *Expensive.* They both knew the Brigham line had fallen well beneath what one might call influential. It was high on the precisely detailed list of reasons she'd pushed him so hard to find an acceptable wife.

He turned to sit in the chair across from her, making certain his feet and elbows were placed in a manner that wouldn't bring a round of censure, although his words surely would.

"Mother, I have doused nearly every woman of high society in my charm since the day I turned two and ten, to no success. They spurn me, every one. They have run off to marry their bakers and their map makers and left me alone in the splendor and finery that the fortitude and fortuitousness of our ancestors bought. There is no one left who meets your standards. I beg you, for the love of all that is tolerable, let this—"

The look she turned on him could have cut glass. In fact, Nickolas felt as if shards of it suddenly lined his spine. He sat straighter, overcome with an urge to check that his vest and cravat were in order.

His mother said coolly, "I have delivered my conditions. You will follow them."

The *or else* was plain in her tone. Nickolas swallowed, knowing full well what the "else" would entail. It wasn't as if he hadn't expected it—they'd been having the same argument for years—but each time he thought of it, the knot inside of him grew tighter. It felt very much as if, if he didn't find a way to stop his mother's plans, the thing that was knotted inside him would become impossible to unbind.

His voice was careful when he told her, "I'm afraid that I cannot do as you've bid." Could not marry. Could not allow himself to be part of her schemes. Could not abide by the underhanded, unpleasant—

The thought cut off at the sound of a knock on the main door. Nickolas's gaze went sharp, but his mother's expression didn't change.

"You speak to me as if I were enfeebled, Nickolas," she said. "I have given you every opportunity to do this on your own. It became clear far before this evening that you cannot."

The knot cinched tighter. He did not know what she'd done. Perhaps the caller was only a lady he was meant to attach himself to. One of his mother's friends, perhaps, in her dotage and desperate for a replacement helpmeet, a stand-in for a dead husband. *Perhaps.* Nickolas stood, wondering if it were too cowardly to leap from the window in escape. His gaze flicked to the balcony. Yes, it would be dangerous and daft and, above all, cowardly. But it would not be the first cowardly thing he'd done.

The light of a bright moon reflecting on the railing brought a sudden, sharp realization of how late it had become. His gaze snapped to his mother. Her face, like that of his eldest sister, was long and slender, her eyes a steely gray. The countenance had been nearly unwavering since the day he'd been born. When the corner of her mouth quirked, he felt his first real shock of fear. It was too late for callers, well past the hour any respectable family would allow themselves presumed not to be abed. And his mother, she had called him there to… Saints, what she had just said.

He did not bother to ask what she had planned; it was too late to attempt any kind of retreat, with dignity or not. He was trapped. Nickolas had known his mother was obstinate, but he had never expected it to go so far. He should have leapt from the window when he'd had the chance.

He straightened, a sense of dread sliding over him as the figures of three hulking men darkened the sitting room door. They were dressed in the livery of castle staff, crisp black suits with very little trim. They were not castle staff. One man met him with a dead-eyed glare. Another's eyes held a concerning amount of twinkle when he rubbed his palms together and said, "Evening, my lord."

"THIS CANNOT BE HAPPENING," Nickolas repeated as they heaved him over a pile of fine silk pillows. It was happening. In fact, most of it already had. The men had hauled him down a darkened corridor, his various attempts at fighting be damned, and into a wing of the castle that held some of the most prominent families in the kingdom, where he'd been unceremoniously dragged through a set of garishly decorated private rooms. His jacket had been torn off in the struggle, his shirt tugged loose over a throbbing side and wrenched shoulder, and now a pair of men with the strength of oxen held him against a sturdy bedpost while a third man tied his hands with his own cravat.

Nickolas hurled a few insults, but he was not quite certain whether they pertained to the henchmen or the woman who had hired them. The men did not seem to care either way. The moment the knot was secure, his captors let go their hold and stepped back to take in their work with the pride only a man of difficult labor could know.

Nickolas let his head drop back against the post, wincing at the pain in his shoulder. "Very well. You've done it. Good job, all of you." He would not tell them what it would cost them, what trusting the lady Brigham would buy them each in the end.

Lashed to the post of a bed in some unnamed lady's room, Nickolas felt they deserved their fate, in any case.

One of the men chuckled. "Aye, a fine job we did. Look at you there, trussed up like a bird."

Another one chimed in, "Fanciest lord I've ever seen, even without his quills."

"Ain't a roasting he's in for." The first one smiled, a row of fine straight teeth flashing in a face that seemed to possess no other symmetry. "Not when Lady Carvell finds him in her bed." The lot of them laughed uproariously, apparently unaware that Nickolas had already begun working the knot.

His mother might have found the men sufficiently brutish and unconcerned with the law to haul him there, but she'd not bothered to make certain they knew their tethering skills. Five more minutes and he would be back in his wing, packing a trunk to leave his mother, his sisters, and if he had to, the entire kingdom of Westrende.

Anything but what she was attempting to set him up for. He would not be forced to marry the Carvell woman, no matter that propriety would demand it.

"There she is now," one of the men whispered as a door in the next room clicked shut. They were gone in an instant, apparently not speaking a word to the woman in the next room on their way out. Beyond the bedchamber door, the sound of light footfalls meandered through the sitting room of the suite. The lady was evidently in no rush, casually about her business before she made her way to the man shackled to her furniture.

In Nickolas's ears was the echo of his mother's words as she'd stood over him while the hired ruffians had prepared to drag him away. "This is for your own good," she had said coldly. "For the good of the family."

Nickolas tore a wrist free of his binds, biting back a curse at the chafing of his skin. He was on his feet, yanking the fabric free, unwilling to leave a single scrap that might be used as evidence against him.

"My lord," a pouting voice called from the doorway. "Don't tell me you're attempting to run away."

Nickolas froze, his back to the woman. He did not turn and did not even look toward the unmistakable sound of Lady Carvell's voice.

Her steps came closer. "My father paid a good deal for this."

There was a low sound in her throat, but it was impossible to guess whether it was anticipation at having him caught or displeasure at his attempted escape. Neither boded well.

"To tie you to me."

Fate save him, the woman had been in on it. She'd not only agreed to the ridiculous plot, but by the sound of it, she'd been eager to marry a man who wanted no part of their scheme. There was a solid chance that when he thought of the scene later, he would be sick. But as he stood, his eyes only scanned the room, searching in the flickering candlelight for any escape.

"Nickolas," she complained. "It's too late for that. By sunrise, everyone will know. You might as well make it easy on all of us."

"My lady," he said, "this will remain, forevermore, between you, me, and that bedpost." His gaze landed on his only recourse. "Predictable," he muttered.

It was the balcony. He should have known; it was always the balcony. Someday, he would be caught in a situation wherein the lady in question lived in a ground-floor room with a dozen windows. Today was not that day.

He rushed toward the doors, thanked every deity he could bring to mind that they weren't locked, and yanked them open to a moonlit night.

A high-pitched scream rent the air behind him. The rush of footsteps that followed was too fast not to have been anticipating the call. He had been right in his guess that a guard waited just outside. It didn't make his choice any easier. Nickolas stared over the balcony railing, his stomach dropping. It wasn't a first-floor room, not even a second. Three stories beneath him waited metal railing, wooden benches, and statuary with more than their fair share of pointy bits. He closed his eyes, vowing to lobby for the installation of more courtyard ponds at the next assembly.

He turned back toward the room, not surprised to find a pair of kingsmen coming through the bedchamber door. What did surprise him, however, was that they were men Nickolas knew—the kingsmen who'd arrested him the last time. Men who had dragged him to a cold, dark cell.

He was done for. The men had thought him guilty of a crime far more dastardly than being in a woman's bed that day and had promised him very bad things. Should they manage to lay hands on him, Nickolas and the Brigham name were through.

He drew a deep breath, swung his legs over the balcony railing, and plummeted into the cool night air.

CHAPTER 2

It was not his finest escape. Nickolas landed unsteadily on a lower stone outcropping, a slanted ledge that, unfortunately, was too slick for proper footing. He slid. He swore.

He fell.

Reaching out, he barely caught hold of a nearby corbel and found his legs swinging with his momentum, then the weight of his body pulled loose his grip. He fell farther, swore again, then crashed against a decorative trellis, where he held on for dear life. It was covered in thorns. Above him, one of the kingsmen shouted.

Below him was a very tall statue of a mostly naked woman atop a rearing horse. He leapt for it and wrapped his arms about the woman's smooth stone neck. He clambered down the rest of her, pausing only briefly to murmur an apology for his grip on her breast. The horse received no such apology. The moment he reached the base, Nickolas threw himself over the surrounding brush and ran full speed out of the garden.

It was late, but the moon was full, illuminating every pale statue and stone barrier. With growing dread, Nickolas spun and ran at every dead end he met in an endless succession of wrong turns. There seemed to be nothing but walls: high walls, low walls, bench walls, topiary walls, and by the Rive, an obscene number of undressed women on horses framed within the surrounding castle walls. He was panting, heart thundering at every sound that might be the kingsmen in pursuit. If they caught him, it was over. All of it, every comfort and freedom he'd ever known.

His life would be ruined. He would have to put on that he'd been in Lady Carvell's bedchamber of his own free will and agree to marry her, or he would be thrown into a cell for breaking into her private suite. He was fairly certain either would bring a special kind of punishment. A woman who would so easily agree to having a man stolen and lashed to her bed against his wishes would certainly not be the sort he would want to bind to his name. But there was more to it than that. Nickolas had encountered the family before; he was acquainted with the woman's father. He knew what the pair were capable of.

A life bound to the Carvell family would be worse than eternity in a dark and lonely cell. At least the kingsmen hadn't jumped down after him. Their lack of senselessness had won Nickolas a momentary opportunity to secure his freedom. While the kingsmen traversed the Carvell rooms to reach the courtyard—avoiding a blind leap into the night like Nickolas—he had one chance to get out.

If only he could find a cursed door.

He stepped on something sharp, swore again, and stumbled forward past a sweetbriar bush. Had he not been looking over his shoulder, he might have noticed the dark metal on the ground in his path. As it was, he did not. Foot tangling in the wires, Nickolas lost his balance and spun, managing to miss falling flat on his face only by taking the packed earth to his back.

A huff of air escaped his chest the same moment that a soft gasp sounded somewhere beyond his head. He glanced up, toward the midnight sky, and whatever breath he'd meant to steal was lost.

Above him, framed by that sky, a face came slowly into view. The creature stared, visage inverted where she knelt over him on the ground. Wisps of rich brown hair curled around a soft, sweet face made pale by the moonlight, her dark eyes impossibly wide. She was a wight, surely, or a statue come to life, some unearthly being that called to mind stories of magic and fae, a being who might capture one's—

"There is no escape."

Her hushed warning cut off whatever his thoughts had been going on about, then the flutter of a dark wing beside Nickolas's head had him bolting to his feet. The woman reached forward to snatch a small gray bird from his path. Her wide, dark eyes traveled up the length of him, his clothes tattered and torn, flesh bared to the night air at his neck and side. Her perusal came to its eventual conclusion when her gaze reached his. Their eyes locked.

The bird flicked a wing, its eyes on him, too, but conveying an eerie level of disdain. Nickolas abruptly recalled the metal that had tripped him and began to yank his foot free of what he realized was a metal cage. He made a sound of annoyed disgust before voices—too near— called him back to the urgency of his flight. His attention snapped to the woman once more. *No escape*, she'd said.

Possibly, she'd meant to imply that she would call the guard —though she hadn't yet screamed—but the ominous warning had not precisely landed as a threat.

He said, "I need out."

Footfalls echoed through the garden, and Nickolas scanned the space, his heart in his throat.

"This is a private courtyard. The only door leads into Lady Carvell's rooms," the woman said. "Or to be more precise, her father's."

Nickolas let out a wheezing, horrified groan.

The corner of her lip twitched. She stood, dusting off a plain, serviceable dress with one delicate hand while holding the drab bird in the other. She was not very tall. She whispered, "Perhaps I can help."

He closed the distance, desperation clear in his entire being. "I beg of you." He prayed she might keep him from spending the entirety of his days inside a prison or, barring that, to at least prevent him from being forced into a marriage with the horrid woman inside those rooms. "Get me out."

Her head tipped back to meet his gaze. "I need something from you. A trade."

"Anything."

She frowned. "You should not agree so readily. You've no notion of my terms."

The sound of boots hitting the path came nearer, not two men now but at least four.

"My lady," Nickolas breathed. "It cannot be worse than the fate I'm facing." At her dubious gaze, he vowed, "Anything."

She gave a sharp nod then turned to face the men just as their chase ended. She slid an arm inside Nickolas's, locking their elbows as if to hold him in place. Had she not, he might have run—had he anywhere else to go.

The kingsmen fell to a stop and took in the scene, their prey standing unreasonably—nonsensically—firm against them, having taken up with a petite maiden and her dingy bird.

"My lady." The stoutest of the kingsmen stepped forward, his head dipping in a bow. "Please step away from this offender so that we might bring him to heel."

"How do you mean?" she asked.

Seemingly taken aback by her casual tone, the kingsman gestured toward Nickolas. "This man is a miscreant, my lady. We've been charged with apprehending him in the name of Westrende."

She glanced briefly at Nickolas. "How odd. What could you think he has done?"

The stout man straightened. Behind him, his brethren shifted impatiently. "It's a private matter, my lady. If you would only step aside—"

She laughed. It was a light, careless thing that seemed to echo off the statues then fall dead in the still night air. "A private matter. Sir, you are surely mistaken about how such business is conducted." She tugged Nickolas nearer while he did his best not to flinch at the proximity of the bird. "Lord Brigham and I are the ones managing a private matter. We are here under the authority of Lord Carvell himself. I wonder that you have the gall to interrupt us." She clicked her tongue in a manner that was neither mild nor good-natured but could not precisely be called out as a challenge. "Do go and leave us in peace."

Despite her words, the kingsman stepped forward. Nickolas moved to pull away, but the tiny woman held firm. He wanted to tell her she was going to be hurt if she didn't let go of him, that the men before them wanted blood. He wanted to tell her to forget their bargain, that she should deny she'd ever encountered him.

"Do you doubt my word?" she asked the kingsman. Her tone turned conversational or perhaps as if she were speaking only to herself. "I wouldn't think so, given my position on chancery staff and my relationship to both the marshal and chancellor. But here you are as if I've said nothing at all."

A spike of ice turned Nickolas's spine rigid. He did not dare look at the woman beside him lest his expression give the shock away. *Chancery. Marshal.* By the wall, he was ruined. He couldn't fathom how he'd stepped into a situation with even more perilous stakes. She was tied to officers of the kingdom. All Nickolas needed now was the presence of the general.

But he was not the only one affected by her remark. A nervous glance darted between two of the kingsmen farther back, and the nearest had frozen in his approach. There was a moment of silence.

"What is going on here?" Lord Carvell's voice rang through the courtyard before he was even in view. He took his time, coat half unbuttoned, cravat hanging loosely at his thick, unshaven neck. Beneath an unkempt brow, his eyes raked the scene with a worrying sharpness. He drew up beside the kingsmen, each of whom had adopted a militant posture, hands on their swords.

Nickolas's shoulders sagged in defeat. When he tried to pull away from the woman, she refused to allow it.

"Lord Carvell," she said in greeting. "How lovely of you to have come to shoo off these men." She made a show of gripping the bird tighter, but her grip was not as tight as the one with which she held to Nickolas.

He was only slightly curious what might happen if they dared try to tear him away from her. Whatever it was, Nickolas understood that she meant him to stay quiet.

"Look what a mess they've made of Frederick's cage."

For one long moment, Lord Carvell stared at the woman before his gaze shifted to Nickolas. Something dark passed over his expression, a sort of slimy self-satisfaction at what he'd done and what seemed to be a promise of what was to follow.

Saints but Nickolas hated that man. "Lord Carvell," Nickolas said with no inclination of his head. "You'll forgive me if I'm not forthcoming with delight at your arrival."

The woman dug an elbow into Nickolas's side. "Because, understandably, we expected the privacy I was promised," she said with a meaningful gaze at the men—a gaze that clearly no one present understood the meaning of at all.

Nickolas cleared his throat to speak, but Lord Carvell, evidently done with the baffling midnight games, jabbed a finger toward Nickolas and barked, "That man is going to walk to my study to sign a contract this instant or be hauled to a dungeon cell to await his trial!"

"A contract?" the woman asked brightly. "Whatever for? You know I love contracts, Lord Carvell. You must tell me. I insist. Don't make me wake the chancellor to find out."

The expression on Carvell's face went hard, his tone final. "Lord Brigham is about to marry my daughter."

The laughter came again, impossible amidst the crowd of stern men and still statues. Nickolas had the sense that if the woman's hand were not occupied cradling a sickly bird, it would have gone to her midsection so she might double over with mirth. "He couldn't possibly," she said with a too-genuine smile.

"Why is that?" Carvell bit out.

"Because." She gazed up at Nickolas. "He's already engaged to me."

CHAPTER 3

Nickolas gaped at the woman beside him. *Engaged*, she'd said. *Chancery*, she'd said. By the wall, he had no idea who the creature even was.

He wondered if that had truly been what he'd agreed to —a marriage with her. He shook off the thought before it could take root, because surely anyone, bird-toting stranger or no, was preferable to a Carvell.

Except he didn't even know her name. He would have liked at the very least to have her name. It was probably an adorable one, something short and cute.

"Brigham!" Carvell snapped, apparently not for the first time.

Nickolas's baffled gaze met his.

"Are you going to stand there and gawp at this woman while she speaks for you?"

Nickolas's palm had somehow found its way to rest over his heart. His other hand was tucked neatly against his middle. The arm it was attached to, beneath nothing but a thin shirt, was still latched to the woman in question.

He wasn't certain who had possession of his jacket, only that it wasn't him.

"Nickolas," Carvell demanded.

Was he going to let her speak for him? To lay out such a blatant deception to save his skin? Nickolas blinked. "Yes, my lord, I believe I am."

The other man's face flamed, every exposed inch of him twitching with fury. "You will beg off this arrangement and marry my daughter this instant."

Beside Nickolas, the woman lifted a shoulder. "We've already filed the paperwork. You'll have to take it up with the magistrate, I'm afraid." On the surface, her tone was conciliatory, but something in it made clear that the woman meant to crush not only Carvell's plans for a marriage but for the arrest as well. She had connections, apparently, and she was not afraid to use them.

Carvell scoffed, his fiery glare darting between the faces of the woman and Nickolas. He noted their posture, the way her slender arm rested possessively inside the crook of Nickolas's elbow. His eyes narrowed. "Lady Brigham would never allow it."

He was right, entirely. Nickolas had no clue who the woman truly was, but her plain dress alone would be enough to cross her off his mother's list. It didn't stop him from clinging to her as his last hope.

The woman gazed up at Nickolas adoringly. The rapid clip of his pulse stuttered.

"Of course," she said in a soft voice. "Which is why we have kept it a secret." When she turned the force of her gaze back to Carvell, her tone was sharp. "Indeed, my lord, it seems best that you keep our news tucked safely near your chest, lest anyone discover what's happened here tonight. As you may recall, even the magistrate was in earshot when you granted permission for my use of this garden. Now, if you'll excuse us, I believe my dear Fredrick deserves a more peaceful courtyard for his home." Her lips tilted consideringly. "Perhaps Lord Keller's garden."

"Yes," Nickolas heard himself say, recalling that Keller was Lord Carvell's greatest rival. The woman glanced back at him, and Nickolas cleared his throat then shook free of whatever foolishness had come over him to focus on Carvell. "It has ponds."

The statement was both a cut and a threat, and with it, Nickolas reached down to retrieve the mangled cage, then he dipped his head to the unknown lady to indicate he was ready to depart. Without another word, they strode from the courtyard of a sputtering Carvell.

THE PAIR MADE it through a dozen castle corridors before reason returned. Nickolas—disheveled and toting a metal cage—and a small woman cradling a dismal bird were rushing through the halls of Westrende as if they'd not just evaded his arrest and announced a betrothal. "Where are we going?"

The woman didn't even spare him a glance. "Your rooms."

She was pulled to a stop as his steps froze, and Nickolas became aware that he still had hold of her. He let go his grip to straighten his shirt and remove a thorn from his sleeve. The bird fluttered a wing.

"We can't very well go to mine," she explained.

Chancery, she'd said. She worked in chancery. Her rooms would be there, right next to the cursed chancellor and every law official in the kingdom.

He stared at her, his hands stilled in their task of restoring his wardrobe to order.

She gestured toward the long, empty corridor. "It's hardly fitting to discuss here."

"It?" His voice seemed to come from somewhere far away.

"Our bargain."

He kept staring, pinned by those big dark eyes, his words barely above a whisper. "Who *are* you?"

She smiled politely. "You may call me Jules." Then she turned, flapping her fingers and chirping, "Come along."

Saints protect him, he did. When they reached the entrance to his suite, the woman—Jules—waited patiently. Nickolas did not unlock the door. Instead, he leaned forward, placing his palm flat against its finely carved surface to peer at her. "My lady, how is it that you knew precisely which door was mine?"

"I work in chancery."

It was no explanation at all. He waited.

She shrugged. "If you'd rather stand draggle-tailed in the corridor, that's perfectly agreeable to me."

He glanced at her skirts, which did not appear at all as if they'd been dipped in mud, despite that she'd been kneeling in the courtyard. She must have been aiming the remark at him, then. "Right. So I should let an unfamiliar woman and her dubious bird into my suite?"

"Frederick is of good character. And you and I..." She

glanced up at him. Those eyes were weapons. "Are betrothed."

Nickolas's forehead thunked against the door. He left it there for a moment then drew a steadying breath. He would do this. If it meant foiling his mother's plans with the Carvells, Nickolas would take the risk of exposing his private life to a stranger with ties to chancery—and her dowdy bird. When he finally straightened to take the key from his pocket, he did not look back at her. "I cannot believe I'm letting fowl enter my sanctuary."

Small cooing sounds came from behind him as Nickolas fired every taper and lamp in the room. He would chase away every shadow in the suite and shed light on every detail of whatever fool bargain he'd agreed to. The woman had warned him, told him not to accept terms he knew nothing of, but he could not fathom how her terms might be worse than what fate had planned for him. He lit the last taper and slid toward the center of his mantel a vase he'd been gifted by a consul, knowing it was time to face her demands.

When he turned, she was standing in the center of his sitting room, her dress the only drab color in the entire brilliant space that was his suite. Well, her dress and that bird. The bird was still glaring at him. He picked up the cage once more, gesturing for Jules to sit while he crossed to a side table to retrieve an ornate letter opener to use as a tool. She chose a low white settee, and he returned to settle across from her, cage in hand. "Tell me about this bargain of yours."

"You don't like birds," she said.

He didn't. He would like very much for one not to be

on his furniture. "This isn't about birds. But while we're on the subject, what were you about in Carvell's courtyard?"

"I've been trying to set him free. Frederick, that is."

Prying a wire straight with the letter opener, Nickolas glanced at the bird cradled in her lap. Clearly, it had an injured wing. "He won't be safe if he can't fly."

She seemed as if she couldn't meet his gaze, her slender fingers adjusting the lay of the bird's wing. "I can't keep him in a cage forever."

"He's fed. He seems loved. Is that not enough?"

"No." The word was not exactly sharp, but it came too fast to pass as indifferent. In a quieter voice, she added, "A creature cannot truly feel loved if it is not free. He must be free before it is too late."

When she finally looked up, Nickolas realized he'd gone still, watching her. He made himself focus once more on the cage. "The bargain. You'll keep me from being charged with breaking into Carvell's rooms, keep him from forcing his daughter upon me, and I'm to marry you. Is that the trade?"

She shifted forward on the settee. "No. Not truly. The betrothal is only a pretense until we are each free of the danger we are in."

The opener slipped from a metal wire to knock against the base of the cage. Nickolas looked up at her.

"You, with the Carvells. And me, with a minor legal issue that I need to resolve posthaste." Her lips shifted into what was likely meant to be a reassuring smile. It failed the task. "The whole thing will be over quickly, I'm certain. We'll be free again before the next moon."

"My lady——"

"Jules," she reminded him. "The marriage won't go

through. I'll submit the paperwork but prevent it from being filed. We don't have to announce it." Her shoulders lifted in a small shrug. "It won't even be a lie. We *have* agreed to the betrothal. We just won't actually carry it out."

"Legal issue," he repeated.

"A trivial matter, really. I would rather not discuss the details."

"With the man you intend to marry."

"Precisely."

"And yet I'm meant to trust you."

The smile she offered next was less reassuring. "Or marry Lady Carvell instead."

Nickolas pressed his eyes shut and drew another breath. "My lady, I need to know this. Whatever danger you are in, I cannot just pretend it away. You have asked me to tie myself in this bargain. At least allow me the courtesy of being aware of the risks we're meant to avoid."

Her smile fell. She seemed to consider her answer for a long moment, one hand coming up to press thin fingers where a pendant might rest beneath the gray cloth. Nickolas did not take his gaze off her until her eyes finally rose to his.

She said, "I need to break a betrothal contract. One that was taken into agreement without my consent and must be broken by someone other than me."

Her parents, then. Not so unlike Nickolas's situation, except she did not appear to have been trussed up for the matter. Though, to be fair, she might have been tied using only less-literal bindings. "You claimed a relationship with both marshal and chancellor," he pressed.

Jules nodded.

"Why not ask them for help?"

Her expression twisted something inside of Nickolas that wasn't the familiar knot that had been set by his mother.

"I cannot," she admitted. "Because I am not a true citizen of Westrende. They would be required by law to return me home. I'd be asking them to break a vow they've made to their kingdom. It's untenable."

She swallowed, the motion clenching that new spot inside of him. Her impossibly wide eyes met his.

"I need you, Nickolas."

The thing inside of him snapped, his heart pulsing strangely as if it might lift from his chest.

It was grounded like a game bird when Jules said evenly, "And if you don't help me, then your only choice is the lady Carvell or a locked cell."

CHAPTER 4

Jules and her bird had left Nickolas with no more than a brief farewell and a list of demands that included an introduction to Lord Beckett—a man who specialized in interkingdom law—and access to the private library of a Brigham family friend. In exchange, she would handle the threat of Carvell and his daughter.

Nickolas and Jules would keep the engagement to themselves.

"Brigham!" William clapped Nickolas on the back. "You're early. Come, have a seat by the best of your associates before that horrific Lady Mena steals in again. I swear the woman's rose water is strong enough to stave off a raging bear."

"And yet it has remained ineffective against you," Nickolas muttered as he scanned the room for any sign of his family, the kingsmen from the night before, or any threat not theretofore anticipated.

William's hand slid to squeeze Nickolas's shoulder, dragging him along to a high row of seats in view of the rostrum where kingdom officials would hold their forum and hear from the lords and ladies of Westrende.

Nickolas tugged himself from the man's grip, settling between Ander and Redmahn instead. He did not have the patience for loutishness today. "Gentlemen."

Ander offered only a brief nod, his eyes on the gathering crowd. Redmahn gave Nickolas the once-over. "Saints, what happened to you? You look as if you slept in the granary again."

"Late night, Lord Brigham?" William said from Ander's other side, far too loudly for Nickolas's taste.

"What are we campaigning for today, my friends?"

"Avoidance will get you everywhere," Ander murmured with a wink. He gestured toward the floor. "Lord Klein is in an uproar about the uptick in kingdom officials being removed from their posts. That's where my interest lies as well. Not to prevent it, mind you. Only to gain some insight so that I might sneak into one of the vacated posts myself."

Nickolas did not reply, because he knew a thing or two about the situation his peers did not. If anything could be said of Westrende, it was that tradition ruled. And it just so happened that tradition called for the willful denial of the existence of magic. It didn't matter that the Rive was in place to keep the kingdom secure, that the ancient wall surrounding it was said to be a border of the fae realm of Rivenwilde. As far as any citizen was concerned, no magic inside Westrende meant no magic existed at all.

Nickolas had once believed the same. He might give anything to go back.

"I'm here to lobby for naked bathing pools," Redmahn announced as he leaned back into his chair.

William made a grunt of disgust. "Not public ones, please. The last thing we need is a bunch of... Saints, that reminds me of the time Lady Carvell went—"

At Nickolas's sharp look, William's words cut off. "By the wall, Nicky, what have I said to upend you?"

"Don't call me that."

His laugh was loud enough to draw looks from the gathering spectators. "Certainly. I'll address you only as the honorable Lord Brigham henceforth. Saints, you're a mess today. What's happened? Some skirt have you riled?"

"Would you *please* keep it down," Nickolas hissed. "A little decorum would not kill you, would it?"

William shrugged. "It might. Best not risk it."

"Speaking of skirts," Ander remarked at a more acceptable volume. "The midsummer ball hits at next week's end. Who can we expect to see on your arm?"

The ball. Nickolas had forgotten. It was a masked affair, another tradition. In days past, a king would mingle with the guests, and not a soul could be certain which was he. No king currently sat on the throne—until one came of age, the council was ruling in his stead—but the ball carried on without him. Every person of status would attend.

It was the perfect chance to introduce Jules to Lord Beckett. The man loathed frippery and never failed to wear the same mask that was no more than a thin strip of fabric barely covering one eye. Nickolas could parade Jules in, right in front of the entire kingdom, and never have to answer about who she truly was.

Redmahn jabbed an elbow into Nickolas's side. "Who is she you're thinking so laboriously of?"

Nickolas's gaze shot to his friend's.

Redmahn laughed. "Oh, a lady has you in her clutches, doesn't she? Whoever she is."

Nickolas shook off the accusation. "I'm only considering the tasks I've to complete this week. Nothing more."

Ander's chuckle was low. "Yes, the contemplation of a busy man. We can all see that."

The gavel banged as the assembly was called to order, and Nickolas was saved from further inquiry. Before him, men and women of the kingdom sat in audience, hearing the concerns and plans that Nickolas was meant to be part of. All he could think of was the ball. He would have to make arrangements quickly, but Jules *had* said the bargain would be over as soon as their complications were sorted. By the next moon, she'd told him. Nickolas could do that. He could take her to a masked gala and let her stay on his arm. His lips drew into a frown, and Nickolas slid his palm over his mouth to keep his friends from noticing. Jules had not appeared to possess the wardrobe for such an event. He could arrange one for her. It would be no trouble.

Besides, the cost of a fine gown would be little expense given that their bargain had saved his hide. The last thing Jules needed to be concerned with was procuring a dress with only days' notice. Being a Brigham afforded him privileges in such matters. He would handle it. He glanced at the grand clock marking the hour. Right after assembly, Nickolas would visit the tailor. And from there, chancery was only a short walk away. She would be thrilled he'd taken initiative, that their bargain would be resolved so expediently.

He needed only to make certain his mother was not aware. Jules would require a particular sort of gown, one that made her seem like the type of lady he might usually have on his arm—but no. She wasn't. He didn't think a gown could do that. Saints, her eyes alone would give her away.

A shout sounded from near the rostrum, snapping Nickolas's attention back to the room, the lords arguing over a tax matter. His gaze roamed the crowd. Far below, across a sea of formal dress, Lord Carvell stared Nickolas down.

Nickolas's lips pressed tighter. The man's look seemed to promise revenge. Nickolas had nothing but the vow of a small woman to save him. Claps and shouts rose through the chamber, but Nickolas and Carvell were still. He would not get up, would not dismiss himself early and let Carvell win.

The Brighams held their ground. That didn't mean they didn't have the sense not to be caught out in an argument before every peer in the realm, though, so the moment the proceedings were through, Nickolas slipped out of the chamber.

NICKOLAS'S TAILOR was a woman sharp only in wit. She had a pleasingly soft manner and person and could be relied upon to dress in a palette of grays that complemented the shade of both her hair and her eyes. She was a woman, he felt, who appeared as if she might pass embraces out as easily as others might offer platitudes. Nickolas adored her.

"Lady Roth." He bowed grandly, despite that she would

never fall for such a thing as easy charm. "So lovely of you to meet with me on short notice."

Her smile was wry. "Lord Brigham, I was never notified at all."

He chuckled. "Alas, here I am. Can you spare a moment for me?"

Gesturing that he follow, she led him past a half dozen seamstresses at work on fine suits and gowns. They arrived into a private room scattered with bolts of silk, where she indicated for Nickolas to take a seat on one of the lush fabric chaises. Lady Roth gave him her full attention.

"I need a gown for the midsummer ball." At the frown she gave him, he explained, "I know it's not much time, but I hope you can help me. Something blue, I think. Not too shimmery. And a mask that covers nearly all of a face. No feathers, please. That's merely a personal preference, not owing to any real requirements on your part. It's for a woman about..." He held his hands in an approximation of Jules's width and height.

Lady Roth gave him a flat look.

In return, he offered a wink. "How's this, then? Something with a sash. We'll just"—his hands gestured again—"draw it tight where the narrow bits are. As good as a custom fit."

"My boy, I've no idea how you've made it to this stage in life without a hint as to how women's garments work. Is there some reason she cannot come here for a fitting?"

Several, but Nickolas would not be admitting them aloud. Deciding against the more easily misconstrued, *It's a private matter, I'm afraid, and I think it best not to parade her through the halls where my mother might see*, he said, "A surprise! I want to gift her something stunning and whisk her off her feet."

Lady Roth did not appear moved.

"Perhaps you're familiar with the lady. She's a clerk's assistant. In chancery. Dark hair. The eyes of a harmless forest creature, though perhaps not-so-innocuous teeth."

"Jules," the tailor guessed.

"There you have it."

"Pretty, peculiar girl, that one."

"Precisely."

"Not your usual type."

Electing to ignore the remark, he leaned forward. "Can you help me?"

She pressed her lips. "I realize that most of the charges do not belong to you personally, but there remains the matter of settling the family's account."

Nickolas's palms slid together, not gracefully. "My lady, one more favor, if I might. I'd rather this purchase was settled off the books."

Her gray eyes narrowed. She would know he was hiding it from his mother, but he wasn't certain if she might guess a reasonable excuse as to why. The truth was out of the question, as it was not reasonable at all.

From the pocket of his vest, Nickolas withdrew a fine gold watch, worth a dozen dresses and matching slippers, then passed it to her. "Will this cover it?"

CHAPTER 5

Nickolas's step was a bit livelier on his way to the chancery. He had a plan. Things were looking up. He was going to find Jules and let her know what he'd done so she might be impressed. No, *prepared*. So that she might be *prepared* to make arrangements for the ball.

"My lord," a passing boy greeted.

Nickolas thought the boy was the cousin of a man his sister was acquainted with. It was a chore to keep up with all the lords and ladies who moved within the circles moving about his circles. But as a Brigham, he had to. One needed to be certain, in any case, when one happened across society, which warranted respect and which a healthy distance. Nickolas gave a vague, moderately friendly reply and tucked his hands into his pockets as he continued his stride. Every kingsman in the hallway made him want to twitch, but only four or so actually had it out for him. The odds were low of running across the wrong one by chance.

Two kingsmen very much not on that list waited outside the entrance to the chancery—where its doors rose high and majestic, despite that it was stuffed to the gills with musty documents and kept closed from too much light or, truly, any fresh air. He should have brought the woman a flower or a token to lighten the place up. He was off his game. He'd never courted a lady he was not actually courting. Because he wasn't courting her.

They were engaged.

He missed a step at the thought then straightened, buttoning his coat and smoothing the front before walking through the entryway. Nickolas threw a smile at the kingsman who gave him a look. "New boots."

The man did not reply. Nickolas cleared his throat quietly and walked on, swallowed up along with the brightness of the castle corridors as his steps carried him into the large, dimly lit, shelf-lined chamber that was the chancery office. Document carts and baskets of scrolls littered the space, long worktables positioned haphazardly throughout. One of the figures bustling about stopped to look at him. "May I help you, my lord?"

The boy was wiry with sandy hair and freckled skin, an air of efficiency practically clinging to his person. Nickolas was fairly certain the boy's name was Robert; he and the other young man assisted with sorting and filing.

"Ah yes, I'm here for—" Nickolas's gaze caught on a petite, plainly dressed figure as it froze with the sound of his voice. His lips slid into a wicked smile. "Her."

Jules turned and faced him, the stack of records in her grip lowering before she placed it firmly on a nearby table. The boy glanced from one to the other but said not a word as he continued his work. Jules closed the distance, her eyes darting once across the chamber before returning to him. "What are you doing here?"

Her tone reminded him that their plan was supposed to remain a secret. "I have news," Nickolas said. "An invitation, in fact."

"Could you not have sent a letter?"

His lips pursed, his hand coming to his chest. He had, in fact, not considered it. "There was not much time to spare. I thought it best I let you know right away."

Beyond her, several rooms back, a dark figure paused inside a narrow doorway—Gideon Alexander, chancellor of Westrende. Nickolas dipped his head in a manner that might be taken as recognition or avoidance, whichever the man preferred. In a low voice, he asked Jules, "Perhaps a garden walk? For privacy."

She frowned then glanced toward the chancellor's office herself. Toward Gideon, she made a gesture that, like his own, might have been a wave of acknowledgment or of warning him off. She brushed a lock of hair back from her temple. "Fine. That sounds... fine."

He put out his arm. "Rarely do I receive such an enthusiastic response. Come, let us walk."

She took his arm and did not glance again at those in the chancery, but her posture did not ease, even when they stepped from the outer corridor and into the warm sun.

"Is this your preferred garden?" he asked. "I quite like the gardens on the east walk. My favorites, though, are just outside, past the Baker cottage and bordering the trees. It is a bit overgrown, to be certain, but I hold that is part of the charm."

She stopped and peered up at him. "Why did you come here?"

"Oh. Precisely." He drew a finely penned invitation from an inside pocket of his coat. "Your introduction to Lord Beckett."

She tugged the card from between his two fingers, the tiniest line forming in the center of her brow as she scanned the words. "This is an invitation to a ball."

"A masked ball," he said with only a hint of smugness. "Where we might appear in plain sight with no one the wiser to our ruse."

Her dark eyes rose to his. "You only moments ago strode into the chancery for all to see."

"Well, I'm an important lord. Perhaps I had documents to file."

Her answering look said that was doubtful.

He ignored the insinuation. He wasn't concerned about agents of the kingdom seeing him. He was concerned about his mother and her society connections, and they didn't bother with matters such as being seen before noon. "This ball will be perfect. Just the thing. And all that's left is a visit to the library. How's tomorrow for that? Or do you have a particular day that you prefer?"

She blinked. "I—yes, tomorrow is well enough. Thank you."

Nickolas straightened. "Prime. Then the matter is practically resolved. By the end of next week, you'll be entirely free of me."

Something in her expression shifted, making Nickolas wish he could steal back the words. But he wasn't certain precisely what he'd said wrong. He had been too flippant, perhaps. She had said she was facing a danger. Maybe the cliff she was standing before was steeper than his own.

"I apologize," he told her. "Etta always says I'm a mule.

I meant no offense. I'm sure your situation is not something you find humor in, and even now, as I offer my regret, I sound impossibly glib."

"No, I—" She shook her head. "I was only thinking."

"Ah." He held out his arm. "Shall we walk, then, while you think?"

Her hand slid inside the crook of his elbow as if automatically, and Nickolas led them at a sedate pace, unspeaking, over the garden path. It was a good garden, boasting lilies and violets and a curving stream that connected several small pools stocked with pike and trout. The far wall was lined with fruit trees, their leaves providing shade to a row of stone benches that sat bookended by sculpted lions at rest.

Jules glanced sidelong at Nickolas.

"Go on. Ask me," he said.

"I don't—"

"Oh, please. We're betrothed. If there are no secrets between lovers, then there certainly shall not be between us as fellow conspirators." He gave her a playful frown, his tone chagrined. "Saints know you've seen about the worst of my character already."

Her lips twitched.

He groaned. "It's worse, then. Not only have you witnessed my latest downfall, but you've heard something even more reprehensible." He closed his eyes and lifted his face toward the sky. "Don't tell me. Lady Asha? The incident with the pig?"

When she didn't answer, he opened one eye to peer at her. "No? Something older, then. Does it have anything to do with a kerchief and three bread rolls?"

She laughed. "Be assured, I've no interest in the details."

He pressed a palm to his chest in a gesture of thanks, and she added, "But you'll recall I did bunk with Lady Ostwind, if only temporarily."

His step faltered. "You—that was you? This whole time?"

"I will admit that I feel flattered not at all. Your reputation was one of unrestrained charm, my lord, yet you did not even recall my name."

He winced. It was likely that Etta had not shared the name, not if she was fond of Jules. And she was fond of her, he realized, because Etta must have taken great care not to mention Jules by name in all of their conversations about her time at the chancery. It was almost offensive.

Nickolas inclined his head in his most gallant manner. "It is my pledge to you now, this day, beneath the sun of a fine Westrende sky, fair Jules who has yet to reveal to me her surname, that your given name, at least, will never fade from my memory, for I will etch it on the very walls of my heart."

"Is your heart made from stone, Lord Brigham?"

He opened his mouth then pressed it shut. "You realize, my lady, that you're meant to merely swoon, not examine the promises made by a suitor."

"Even once we are betrothed?"

His expression went grave. "Especially then."

"I'll take it under consideration."

"I think it's in the vows." He paused. "You should not examine those, either."

"Sage advice. You realize I work in the chancery office? With records and contracts?"

"Mmm."

"Indeed."

"My lady." He gave her a look. "Jules." When her smile teased *you remembered*, he flashed a grin before letting it melt into something more solemn. "You haven't asked."

They reached the end of the garden, and she turned. Nickolas turned with her. Farther up the path from where they'd come, a dark-haired man sat in the dappled shade of a willow, his gaze on the nearest pond. "You made suit for Antonetta," Jules said.

Nickolas let out a breath. "Not officially, no. But I did think we would suit." They had been friends since they were children. He knew her. Trusted her. If anyone could have stood against his mother, it would have been Etta. But she wouldn't have had to, because her family was among the highest of Westrende. "She would have done well in the position."

"Done well?" Jules asked. "You sound as if you're hiring staff."

She wasn't wrong. The qualification for the position was *satisfy Nickolas's mother without being crushed by the force of it*. He said, "Fortunately for us all, she held not a whit of interest in taking the post." After a moment, he added fondly, "She always was a bit of a bully, so there's that."

"It seems as if you care for her a great deal."

"I do. Antonetta is like the sister I never had."

Jules's brow crinkled. "I was under the impression you had four sisters."

He made a sound of agreement in his throat. He tried not to speak poorly of his sisters, but the truth was they were more his mother's daughters than anything else. They might be Nickolas's blood, but they were certainly not of the same heart.

Nickolas and Jules were silent for a long while as they walked. They would soon be at the edge of the garden, where he would have to return her to the chancery. Voice low, he said, "My lady, you may ask me whatever it is outright."

She glanced up at him.

"The thing that you wished to draw from me by inquiring of Lady Ostwind."

Her expression fell a bit. "You have quite a reputation for trying for a bride, yet you remain unmarried. It is certainly not for lack of status or charm." He pressed his lips, and she asked, "Have you never truly wanted any of them? For yourself?"

For yourself, she'd said. Because Jules understood the situation with Lady Carvell had been created by Nickolas's mother. But she would not know the extent of it. Not even close.

He could not tell her that wanting someone, that caring for them at all, would be precisely the sort of reason that made it impossible to try. He could never tie a decent person to such an indecent situation. He could not allow someone he cared about to be used in his mother's game.

He couldn't make himself tell Jules that, so he asked, "Have you?"

A shadow crossed her expression, unfathomable in its depth. An instant later, the evidence of her grief was gone, but the memory of it remained with Nickolas. It had been like a knife to the heart.

Jules said, "I have great love for... my many..." She shook her head. "I cannot speak of it." She offered him a shaky smile, her free hand lifting to press at what must have been a pendant hidden beneath the fabric of her gown, though he could see only its chain. "I've had too much love in my life. There isn't room, I'm afraid, for more."

They reached the end of the path. Nickolas faced her, laying his hand gently over hers where it rested on his arm. "Allow me to assure you, then, that there is no one you can trust more than I not to intrude on your too-generous heart."

He dipped his head, drawing her hand to his lips to press a soft kiss on her skin. He glanced up at her. "May we both enjoy the safety of our most fitting betrothal yet."

A warning flashed in her gaze, and Nickolas straightened to follow where it held over his shoulder. The man down the path had stood and faced them, his eyes narrowed on the delicate fingers in Nickolas's hand.

"Nickolas," Jules urged. "Come along. It's time to return to the chancery."

CHAPTER 6

Nickolas was still contemplating the man from the path as he walked away from the chancery entrance. It had been strange, but Jules had not seemed afraid. The only urgency, it seemed, was to remove herself from Nickolas's company.

He frowned, disliking the idea, and turned the corner into a connecting corridor, where he was met directly with the worst thing he could possibly imagine—his mother's narrowed gaze. He was not proud when he made a small startled yelp and stumbled backward.

Her jaw was set. "Who was that?"

Internally, Nickolas cursed. Outwardly, he only blinked in confusion. "Who?"

Her tone lowered dangerously. "That chit you just left. Do not try me, boy."

He made to brush past her. "I've no idea what you're on about. I was at the chancery to see Gideon."

She put a hand on his arm as if to stall him. "You loathe Lord Alexander."

"Yes." He made a show of sighing. "But Antonetta has asked that I make the effort. So I have, for her."

A kingsman passed in the connecting corridor, and his mother snapped, "Come with me."

"I do not believe I will."

Her fingers curled into the material of his coat, warning him not to disobey her again.

Nickolas felt his expression go hard. He leaned in. "The Carvells, Mother? Really? Have you entirely lost your mind? To have your own son trussed up like a—"

Another figure passed in the corridor, and Nickolas dropped his voice. "You know what Lord Carvell is capable of. You know the sort of man, the sort of family you were trying to tie us to. Has it truly come to this? Have the Brighams fallen so low?"

"They have fallen precisely so low. And you will bring them back. I do not know how you managed to wrangle out of the arrangement, but mark my words, you will regret this defiance. If you know what is best for you, for the Brigham name, you will make things right with the Carvells." Each word she spoke was bitten off with too-sharp teeth. Carvell might have heeded Jules's warning to keep the incident in the garden private, but it was clear Nickolas was not yet safe.

He tugged his jacket from her considerable grip. "*Right* is evidently the only direction absent from your moral compass. Now, if you'll excuse me, Mother, I have business to attend."

He strode from her, the ire in her gaze tightening the knot in him until he felt rather like he might be sick. He'd made a mistake. He'd been convinced his mother would be nowhere near. She must have heard that he'd escaped her ambush and come to discover how for herself. Nickolas couldn't stand to think of the position he'd put Jules in. If his mother discovered their ruse, if she tried to hurt Jules or to remove her from Nickolas's life...

So help him, he would never marry if he could help it. He hadn't been worried about Etta. She was stubborn and strong-willed, and she possessed a high-enough station that she would have at least had the chance to hold her footing against his mother. But Nickolas could not subject any other woman to his situation or his mother. He needed to sever her attempts to control him. He had to find a way to escape for good.

Whatever Nickolas did, he would have to do it fast. The longer he lingered, the greater the chance he took that someone would get hurt.

NICKOLAS WAS NO MORE than another single corridor away before he was tweaked by the ear and dragged through a nearby doorway. He jerked away from the grip just as the door was slammed shut, closing him in a narrow room with Lady Antonetta Ostwind.

Nickolas rubbed his ear. "That was uncalled for."

Etta leaned toward him. "Was it?" She was in uniform, her hair drawn back and her manner firm.

"Don't you have work to do?" he groused.

She crossed her arms. "Yes, in fact. I was doing it when I caught sight of Lord Nickolas Brigham prancing after a member of chancery staff like a hobbledehoy."

Nickolas drew back. "I was not."

"You were. I cannot believe you, Nickolas. Marriage? To Jules?"

His protestations fell flat. He should have known she would find out. Maybe he had known she would, in truth, though he would have thought it might take a bit longer than a single day.

"It's public record," she reminded him. "Anyone can see it."

"Anyone who looks. And why were you looking? No one reads the records filed with chancery." He narrowed his gaze. "Did Gideon tell you?"

"How I found out is beside the point. What are you thinking?"

He leaned on a small table near the wall. "What's so wrong with it? You think I'm so unfit that I couldn't please a sweet, gentle-mannered lady? That I deserve someone hideous and uncouth?"

"Sweet?" Tone incredulous, Etta lifted her hands to the room as if displaying his statement as evidence. "You clearly know nothing of her at all. Jules has never been one to trifle with. But that's not the issue." Her hands dropped, and she took a calming breath. "She's a stranger to you. She does not belong in your world. It's a bad match, Nickolas, and you know it. Have things become so desperate—"

He straightened. "Don't. Don't pretend you understand what it's like to need a match. You, who spent your entire existence determined to do everything on your own. Honestly, Antonetta. I'm offended." He met her gaze. "I know I'm not good enough for her. I'm certain she knows it as well. Our agreement is temporary. That's all. Just to keep..." He sighed and slumped against the table once more. He was a grown man; he could not bring himself to say *to keep my mother at bay*. "I was caught in Lady Carvell's room. Her father meant to force my hand, and Jules saved me. Nothing more. I'll leave her be, just as soon as I'm able."

Etta flopped down on a bench, fingertips pressing to her temples. "Carvell? Saints, Nickolas, what have you done?"

Lips pressing down, he said, "The usual, I suspect." The thing everyone expected of him. The worst, most rakish and irresponsible thing. He let out a long breath. "I'll make it right with Jules. Then I will leave her alone. I swear it."

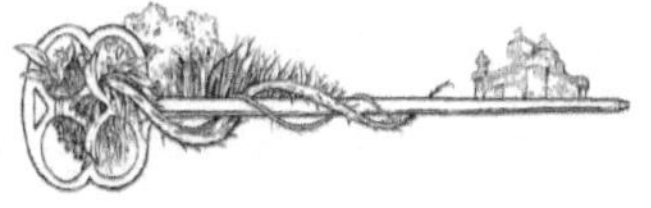

CHAPTER 7

After being accosted by both his mother and Antonetta, Nickolas had sent a missive to Jules to arrange their meeting for the following day—at a lesser-used entrance near the mews instead of anywhere they might easily be seen. The Filmore family library, it turned out, was not inside the castle at all but at a private estate near the far walls of the kingdom. It explained why Jules had not been able to secure her own invitation. Their caper—for that was somehow what it felt like—would occupy the entire day.

The early-morning sun was bright and warm and making Nickolas feel quite impatient as he waited for Jules's arrival near the massive stone archway outside the castle. He examined the toe of a boot, straightened his vest for the dozenth time, then forced his hands into his pockets. A fine script was carved into the stone beneath his feet, a motto of the kingdom: *Within these walls, justice*. He'd been taught it as a boy and recited it so often that the words barely meant anything at all. Now he wondered what the motto might mean regarding what waited outside of the kingdom walls.

It had not seemed to keep the fae from attempting to meddle in kingdom affairs. Rivenwilde and its prince were the greatest threat to the kingdom's safety. The desire to deliver justice upon the fae had driven Etta to become marshal. It was also the reason so many Westrende officials had been removed from their posts.

When Nickolas glanced up, Jules was finally walking toward him, her slight form fitted into a dark-gray gown nearly identical to the shade of her bird.

Nickolas's restlessness immediately ceased. She had brought the bird. To visit a library.

Her eyes were on him, watchful.

He dipped into a bow. "My lady Jules." To the bird, he said, "Frederick."

"I hope you don't mind," she said. "I cannot leave him alone, and Robert and Tobias were occupied."

"Not at all." Just beyond the entrance and down a short set of stairs, their carriage waited. There, Nickolas would be trapped inside a confined space for the better part of an hour. With a bird. He cleared his throat. "Any friend of yours and all that." He held out an arm, forcing his gaze away from her bare neck, revealed by hair that was swept up into an intricate knot. A gold chain rested against her skin, whatever hung from it hidden where it dipped into the bodice of her gown. He glanced determinedly toward the sky. "Should be a lovely ride. We have the weather for it."

She made a small hum of agreement.

When they reached the carriage, Nickolas took the cage, Frederick's dark bird-eyes on him as Nickolas climbed in to secure the wire contraption to one of the bench seats. He'd meant to go back for Jules, but she took the footman's hand and stepped up after Nickolas, forcing him backward into a seat. She did not use the bench holding the cage but instead slid in beside Nickolas. He straightened, drawing himself against the wall so that she might have more room. The faint scent of violets rose from her, along with a trace of something that he could not quite make out. Nickolas resisted the urge to lean closer. He was all but pressed against her as it was.

Across the carriage, Frederick glared.

The footman closed the door, and in short order, the carriage juddered to a start. The sound of hoofbeats on cobblestones fell into a rhythm, and Nickolas eased against the cushioned seat back. Outside the window, men on horseback shifted in the shadows of narrow passages, watching the elaborate conveyance roll by. Their gazes slid away one by one at Nickolas's attention.

"What is it that so unsettles you?" Jules asked, drawing his focus from the men. At Nickolas's look, she gestured toward the cage. "About birds."

He regarded Frederick. "Must I have some tangible reason? A horrific accident as a boy or traumatic history involving the creatures that prevents me from enjoying their company? Some very specific incident that tortures me to this day?"

She watched him.

"I do not." He attempted to cross his arms, brushed an elbow against Jules, then dropped his hands to his lap. It should have been enough that the creatures were unset-tling. Frederick, in fact, took the act to another level. His eyes were black but not at all hollow. Intelligent, dark, and... oddly judgmental. Focused too sharply on one particular person. Nickolas shuddered. "I reserve my right to the opinion."

Jules's face turned toward the window but not before he'd seen the way she bit her lip.

"What is so great about birds, in any case? Of all the pets from which to choose, why a feathered—" He caught himself before an expletive escaped, then cleared his throat.

She chuckled. "That is a considerable dislike you possess, my lord."

He leaned nearer. It couldn't be helped. "What is your second-favorite pet, then? Perhaps I will like that."

"When I was a girl, I was given a menagerie of sorts."

"A menagerie, was it?" He imagined young Jules with a heap of some small furry things. Mewling kittens, perhaps. Or rabbit kits, whatever noise they made.

She hummed in agreement. "I was denied sweets for a month when I set the lot of them free. It was made quite clear afterward that I would not be allowed a pet until I was of age and under my own care, which I'm afraid illustrates that my father missed the point entirely."

"Ah," Nickolas purred. "A criminal from the start. As I suspected."

"Who is to decide what is criminal? The act was misguided perhaps, but not the intention behind it. No creature wants for a cage."

"Indeed," Nickolas said. "Compassion is a great virtue. Even if one does choose to bestow it upon a wounded bird."

"Compassion can be bravery when one opens their heart to what they fear."

"I would not go as far as calling it *fear*," he hedged.

"Nor could we call it unflinching."

"Touché. And what of you?" he murmured, trying terribly not to stare at the line of her neck. "Is there nothing that unsettles you?"

She looked back at him, all hint of humor gone from her expression. "Yes. A great many things, Lord Brigham."

Nickolas regretted that he had asked. "Very well," he said, attempting to step back from whatever precipice loomed over their conversation. "Then we shall each have and keep our dislikes."

The edge of her lip shifted but not into a true smile. Nickolas fell silent, hating whatever dark emotion hid behind her reaction, and they both took to watching the kingdom pass outside.

It was warm inside the cabin, and the early sun came bright through the carriage windows. He felt Jules lean into him after a bit, away from the light that shone more heavily on her side. He made no comment, but after a while of silent stillness, he glanced over to find that she'd somehow drifted off to sleep. He stared at her motionless form, the way her limbs seemed to have gone entirely loose and the way her shoulder pressed to his, all hint of distress erased from her features. Her head canted toward him, rocking with every bump and jostle. He wasn't certain whether he should move but knew her position must be uncomfortable. He shifted, only barely, to allow her form to fall further against him, catching her head against the shoulder of his jacket without having to touch her more than she had done on her own.

Satisfied, Nickolas returned his gaze to the seat before them. Frederick perched in his cage, birdy glare intensified.

Nickolas resisted the impulse to reply. As if being judged for his behavior with ladies by the entire court was not enough, he was suddenly being outclassed by fowl. He purposefully returned his attention to the carriage window.

The trip carried on, taking them past the many shops and residences, winding through the narrow streets inside Westrende's border, until their way widened with more distance from the kingdom center. Nickolas had loved escaping as a boy, had adored the sense of freedom that came with being outside the castle walls. It was more than simply the expanse of pasture and open sky. It was the space created by the very lack of courtiers.

It was the way it had made him feel as if he might finally breathe.

Etta had held little patience for him then—perhaps not a great deal more than she had in later years—because her entire being was molded around the kingdom and its structure. Her father had been no kinder than Nickolas's mother, but the pair of them had found their contentment in entirely different directions. Nickolas and the other boys had run and screamed and flung caution—and propriety—to the wind when they were away. He'd returned so often without his coat—and on one particularly shameful occasion, his trousers—that Nickolas's mother had punished him by way of making him work off his debt with Lady Roth.

His days mending tools and carrying crates for the tailor had been some of the most enjoyable of his youth. It was the single day he'd been relegated to the bird lady's care that he refused to dwell on. The last thing he would ever do was admit the story to Jules and her censorious bird.

The carriage passed beneath a massive gateway, and Nickolas glanced at Jules. They were nearly at the Filmore estate, and she'd settled quite firmly against him. She was altogether adorable when she was sleeping, not a hint of her sharp, graceful movements in sight. One slippered foot was turned outward, the other tucked beneath the bench. Her hand had curled into the hem of his coat, like a child with a familiar blanket, and her cheek was plastered to his arm. He should wake her. He didn't want to.

He ducked his head toward hers to whisper news of their arrival, but somehow, unfathomably, his lips found their way to brush softly against the crown of her head.

Jules moved.

Nickolas started, straightening, in utter disbelief at what he'd done.

Across the carriage, the bird squawked in outrage then glared what had to be a threat of death.

Nickolas kept his eyes on the creature regardless as, beside him, Jules blinked awake.

Stretching her arms surreptitiously, she glanced out the carriage window. "Here already?"

He cleared his throat, gaze pinned to the unmistakably livid bird. "Yes, just."

Jules ran her delicate fingers over her hair, sweeping back the few strands that had gone astray as she took in the bird. "Good. By the look of it, I don't think Frederick enjoys carriage rides."

"NICKOLAS!" chirped the tall blond woman who met them in the grand entrance room at the Filmore estate.

Nickolas bowed deeply. "Lady Filmore. Lovely to see you again."

She rushed forward and took his hand in hers before performing a dip that displayed bare arms and a great deal of silk taffeta skirt.

"Compliments on your gown, my lady." He stepped back, but Lady Filmore gave him no distance, keeping hold of his hand while he gestured toward Jules where she stood with her bird. "May I introduce the lady"—he pressed his lips, giving Jules a wink to remind her of his carved-stone heart—"Jules."

Jules dipped briefly. Lady Filmore stared blankly at the cage in Jules's hand.

"And this is Frederick," Nickolas said. "He ranks higher than a mere lord, I believe, though I've yet to gather his full heritage. Has the bearing for royalty. A prince at least."

At his jest, Jules made a choked sound.

Lady Filmore only blinked.

It was progress, he supposed. Nickolas cleared his throat, giving Lady Filmore's hand a little squeeze to remind her that she'd not let go and was not exactly welcoming her guest. "Allow me to extend my gratitude, again, for the favor your family has bestowed upon us today. I assure you that it is most appreciated and will not soon be forgotten."

"Of course," she replied automatically, evidently taking her eyes off the cage only so they might travel over Jules's gown with a no-less-forgiving expression.

Nickolas pulled his hand from Lady Filmore's grip then offered his arm to Jules. "The estate is lovely, as always,

Lady Filmore. You must convey my admiration to your father. Such an esteemed property and kept so well by your family."

Lady Filmore's eyes met his, the woman finally taking up his reminders of civility. "Yes. It is lovely. Particularly this time of year. I hope you'll join us for the annual gathering in the gardens, Lord Brigham."

"You must" came another voice from the entrance to the room. Another Filmore sister, dressed nearly identical to the first. "Promise us now before the midsummer ball, where you might be swayed into more lofty pursuits. Rumor has it there will be a handful of all-too-intriguing visitors present. I do so hate to be overshadowed."

"Lady Filmore." Nickolas offered a bow. "We were just headed to the—"

"I know," said the elder sister. "You must permit me to escort you." She also made to reach for his hand, but one glance at Jules—and the cage—and the elder Lady Filmore called for the butler. "Take this contrivance away, please." The sound she made could be classified as nothing but disgust.

Jules drew the cage closer. "Frederick stays with me."

The butler, under direction from his employer by means of a less-than-subtle look, persisted. His hand closed over a bar. The bird drove its beak into the man's fingers. Jules did not let go.

Nickolas moved forward, but neither of the pair spared him a glance. "Lady Filmore," Nickolas said levelly, "kindly instruct your man to remove himself from my lady's presence before I do it for him."

The elder sister laughed, the sound too cheery and

overloud in the open chamber. "My lord, surely you do not intend—"

At his look, she apparently understood he *did* intend, because she called the butler down. The lot of them stood in the near silence for one long moment, broken only by the complaints of the aggrieved bird.

Nickolas adjusted his lapel then gave a sharp nod before tugging on Jules's arm, submitting not a moment more to the sisters. Tension remained in Jules's grip on the cage, then they were in the library and safely out of conflict's way. It was the better part of an hour before either spoke another word, and when they did, it was not in regard to how she'd been treated.

"May I help you find whatever it is that you are looking for?" Nickolas finally asked as he watched Jules from where he leaned on a nearby set of shelves.

"I can't—" she started, a tightening in her expression seeming to cut short the words. She shook her head. "I have to do it myself."

He picked up a small ceramic container, halfheartedly examining the painted vines circling its lid. He was fairly certain it was imported, but he'd seen impressive enough imitations. Every summer, there was a little stall set up near the gate with one of the traveling markets, where a family of painters possessed a remarkable talent to mimic nearly any style. Nickolas had always marveled at the courtiers who passed by the youngest child's original gems in favor of lesser works in a popular fashion. "And we are not to ask the Filmore—"

Jules shot him a look.

He could not help but bite back a smile. "Yes, you told me." His fingers twisted at his lips before performing the act of throwing away an invisible key. "They must never know."

Nickolas turned to the shelf, gaze blurring over a dozen embossed titles bound in leather. "It's only that it seems more expeditious to use me. After all, I am here."

Jules stopped in the motion of sliding a slim volume back into its spot to look at him. "Perhaps you should find a diversion to occupy your time."

"Perhaps," he said, chastened. Glancing about the room, he thought that there was not particularly anything more diverting than watching Jules at her work. The thought had him certain it was time to find an alternate occupation. He strode away from her, crossed to an entirely different section of books, drew one from the shelf at random, and took it to the far end of the room, where sunlight fell over a lovely trio of lounges.

He reclined onto one and opened the book. He managed more than an hour of reading before his eyes began to lift once more, catching on Jules where her search had progressed to shelves nearer to him. Restlessness beginning anew, he closed the book, wandered toward the window, then found himself seated at the pianoforte.

He was rarely idle, no matter the reputation he'd earned, and being trapped inside any space for long made a desire to climb the walls rise up in him. He'd had enough wall climbing, he reminded himself, fingers dancing along the keys with a favorite sonata.

When Jules sauntered closer, he glanced sidelong to discover she was watching his hands. He found himself shifting into a more complicated piece, and the set of her mouth shifted with it. He teased, "What have you to say, fair maiden whose name I wear etched on my heart?"

Her dark eyes slid to his. "For one who so dislikes birds, you do a great deal of preening, Lord Brigham."

Nickolas's playing broke off. He turned to her where she stood, too near his perch on the delicate embroidered bench. "You think me displaying my plumage, then."

Her gaze moved meaningfully toward his hands.

He held them up for her inspection. "These?" It felt oddly dangerous, playing this game. He knew precisely what she was implying. He *had* kept on with the playing to impress her. He couldn't seem to stop himself.

"Yes, those. You wave them about as if baiting a fish."

He stared at her.

"Everyone knows what you're about."

Nickolas attempted to appear as innocent as possible. "Ladies have a preference for capable hands?"

She gave him a level look. It was particularly level, as he was sitting and she was standing before him, finally bringing them eye to eye.

He leaned into a more casual stance, one foot sliding forward. Toward her. "Forgive me, my lady, but how else am I meant to catch a wife?"

If color touched her cheeks, he could not see it, because Jules turned away and resumed her perusal of the books. She had not moved far, though, only paces from where he sat. "Perhaps they are not falling for you because your interest is clearly not genuine."

Perhaps he didn't really want to bring them into his life.

"Perhaps," she continued, "you might aim instead for one who doesn't care only for fancy feathers."

He scoffed. Jules did not take the opportunity to say more, despite that he'd crossed a boundary already.

He watched her silently, the sunlight catching on her

dark upswept hair before she shifted farther into the shadows. When she reached as if to draw a book from an upper shelf, too far above her, Nickolas stood. He stepped behind her, one hand brushing her waist to still her as his other slipped past hers to draw the book from its place. He lowered the volume, and Jules seemed to hesitate before taking it from his hand.

Saints, she smelled faintly of violets, of sun-warmed books, and the bare skin of that elegant neck was only a breath away from his, from his own breath because he was practically panting on her, for the love of—

He stepped back. Cleared his throat. "A repast," he heard himself say. "We've been inside far too long. Let us take a break, go outdoors, and rest your eyes before returning to work."

Jules glanced back at him, clearly unhappy at the prospect.

"Only for a bit. We can come back straightaway, and if you do not find your answers today, we will return again until you are satisfied." When she looked doubtful, he added, "Think of the bird. Poor Frederick needs some air."

From his cage atop a table by the chaise, the bird squawked in contempt.

Nickolas gave Jules a look to imply her creature was in agreement and felt warmth cut through the knot inside him at the hint of her sardonic smile. "It is agreed, then." He held an arm forward to lead her from the seeming confines of what was, truly, an impressively spacious room.

The Filmore gardens were absolutely lovely, some of the best the kingdom had to offer, and it took no time at all for the fresh air and bright sun to bring a pleasant languor to both Jules and Nickolas. Frederick, however, adopted an even surlier demeanor. Jules had taken the bird from his cage and placed him gently in the grass beside the spot where they had spread their meal. The creature stared on, mostly at Nickolas, refusing both the coddling and bread his mistress offered, wings tucked tightly to his sides and complaints rattling loudly from his chest.

It was evident his discontent weighed on Jules, but no matter her coaxing, the bird refused to move away. She'd been trying to set him free, she'd said before. Nickolas wondered at the pair, as clearly Jules might just leave him should she want badly enough for him to be free, injured wing notwithstanding. But Nickolas did not wish to pry into a situation that seemed so unlikely to end well for either the bird or his caregiver. "The Filmores keep no predators in this garden," Nickolas said. "You may rest easy on that front."

Jules leaned onto an elbow, just as she'd been convening with the bird, then sighed and laid her head on her arm.

"Your eyes are heavy," he said. "You've time to rest."

"I have no time," she told him. "That's the problem. Time is spending faster than I can…"

There was an unmistakable tremble to her words as they trailed off. He wondered why she seemed so weary despite her nap in the carriage. Perhaps her worries had brought sleepless nights. But it seemed nothing should trouble her in such a fine sunlit garden, someone to watch over her while she slumbered. "Come." Nickolas opened an arm so that she might lie against him instead of the ground. "Troubles only grow larger when one's in need of rest. You may tackle it after. Half an hour will not break you."

She eyed him warily. "Ten minutes."

He felt the edge of his lip tilt and gestured her closer with his outstretched arm. "I'll take care to wake you precisely then."

Having Jules snuggled against him in the warm sun untied the knot inside of Nickolas before the first few minutes were up. His own eyes became heavy, his arm gone limp around her, and the small garden sounds a lullaby to his ears. So when, sometime later, Jules shrieked, he startled from sleep like the world had exploded around him.

"Frederick!" she shrieked. "Frederick is gone!"

Chest heaving, Nickolas stared at the display of absolute terror in a person whose manner had seemed nearly unshakable in the face of greater foes. He stood, glancing around the bare spot of green they'd settled upon and landing on an empty cage. A dull-gray feather was all that remained where Frederick had posted himself in his earlier refusal to move. Dread sank in Nickolas's gut.

"We'll search the surrounding vegetation. If he left on his own, he can't have gotten far."

"I've already searched," she said. "And what do you mean *left on his own*? You said there were no predators here!"

He pressed his lips. The bird's wing was too damaged; he could not have flown. There indeed was no sign of any other animal that might have approached. There was, however, a patch of matted grass in a size more like that of a human boot. "I'll request aid from the Filmores." If one of the ladies had played a prank, he would ensure they answered to their father for it, but Nickolas would find that bird.

Jules glanced at the manor, its wide row of high windows overlooking the garden. "There," she said. "It will offer a vantage point of the entire space." She grabbed Nickolas's arm, and they moved toward the house with an urgency that drew attention. From both the upper and lower floors, Nickolas could see figures taking note of their approach. Inside, he gave direction to a member of the staff, and Nickolas and Jules were up the steps in a rush for the high windows. If they didn't see anything of use, he would leave her there and go find Lord Filmore himself.

Nickolas was so set in his course that when they topped the final staircase and turned to find a gathering of figures, he stopped cold, entirely motionless, to stare in shock.

At his mother.

Jules's step faltered a moment later, her gaze trailing from the stately woman centered before a balcony railing to the dark-clothed beast of a man at her left then the dark-clothed brute of a man on her right.

"Mother," Nickolas managed. "What are you doing here?"

She gave him her most haughty countenance. "I might ask the same of you." Her gaze flicked briefly toward Jules, only long enough to convey that the woman was utterly beneath contempt.

Nickolas stiffened. "We do not have time for this." He might have hissed *and on Filmore grounds, no less?* for the woman had clearly lost her senses. She'd taken to kidnapping and trespassing in order to see her wishes fulfilled.

But they truly did not have the time. He took hold of Jules's arm to lead her away. They had to find—

He froze again as his mother flicked a hand. Nickolas recognized the gesture; it was one he'd experienced countless times before. It spoke of retribution, and what swiftly followed was always the punishment for his disobedience. What came instead was far worse than any injury she'd offered before, because it would hurt not only Nickolas.

"I suspected you might say as much." His mother's tone was cold as the man beside her drew an object from inside his coat. "Which was why I have provided incentive."

A chill silence swallowed the room, its bright windows and open space doing nothing to dampen the severity of the threat. Gripped within a cage of the giant man's fingers was the stout feathered mass of a dull-gray bird.

"*Frederick.*" The word wheezed out of Nickolas, no disguise to his disbelief. Nickolas's attention snapped to his mother.

Her expression held no remorse. "You will leave off whatever shameful foolishness you're about with this girl and agree to marry Lady Carvell. Or you will both suffer the consequences." Her tone made clear the consequences did not end there.

He took a step forward. The man shifted to hold the bird over the balcony.

Nickolas went rigid. Frederick's wing was broken. He would not survive the fall.

Beside him, Jules stepped forward. "I warn you not to do that," she said. Her words were only for the man, with no hint of acknowledgment for Nickolas's mother.

"Shouldn't have left your man behind," the brute on Lady Brigham's other side said. "Don't think you'll have much luck at stopping us on your own."

Her man. The one who'd approached when he'd kissed Jules's hand must have been a guard. But he didn't understand *why* Jules would have a guard. Nickolas glanced at her, but Jules's attention was only on the beast holding her bird.

"What happens to you as a result will be worse than you can ever imagine," she told the man.

There was such surety in her tone that even Nickolas felt uncertain, but his mother's man was under orders. The beast glanced nervously at Lady Brigham. The lady in question said to Nickolas, "Agree now, or this will be the least of your worries."

"I am your only son."

"And I would never harm you." Her brow lifted as she slid a glance toward Jules.

Nickolas would not stand for it. "This has nothing to do with her, Mother. I will not allow you to hurt her. Understand that she is without fault. Lady Carvell, however—"

His mother's hand flicked again. The three figures at the railing turned.

Before another movement could be made, the beastly man tossed the bird over the balcony rail.

Nickolas lunged just as Jules whispered a single word.

The scene stopped dead, the world gone unnaturally still and Nickolas catching himself mid-dive as a man-shaped shadow shimmered into view. Suddenly, before them, angled away from the turned backs of Lady Brigham and her men and looking on where Nickolas watched with Jules was an unmistakable figure swathed in nebulous black.

The prince of Rivenwilde.

CHAPTER 9

Jules had called upon a fae prince. In the Filmores' manor. Right upon their balcony floor.

Nickolas pressed the base of his palms over his eyes.

He could see the fae, just as the tales had always warned. *Lay eyes upon him, and the shadows will clear.* He wouldn't see only the single man. He would see all fae, every creature. He would be tied to their world. A sad, desperate noise crawled from his chest. He drew his hands away to look accusingly at Jules.

"The prince of the Riven court," he said dreadfully.

She did not answer, despite that it had sounded more a question than anything else. Her eyes were on the prince.

Nickolas turned to look at him as well, never mind that he had in no way wanted to see. That he still wished he could not. Tall and slender, with dark hair and darker eyes, the man seemed elegant, regal, and entirely unnatural. Nickolas took a step in front of Jules. She stepped out from behind him.

Taking in the scene—Nickolas's mother and her lackeys and, *by the wall*, that awful bird, frozen in position in a way that made Nickolas's stomach pitch and senses whirl—the fae prince seemed unsurprised by it all. He turned and looked at Jules, the light catching on the spiky crown of tangled bone upon his head.

It was clear the prince understood what had transpired. To Jules, he asked, "Shall I just—" He made a flicking gesture as if to knock Lady Brigham and her henchmen over the ledge.

Jules shook her head. "No, just save Frederick."

"The bird," the prince said. "That is all?"

"No!" Nickolas shouted, more to the room in general than specifically at Jules. "Have you lost all sense? Don't bargain with him. He's the *prince of Rivenwilde*. You must not be tied to him."

"It's too late for that." There was something hard in Jules's reply, something Nickolas had never heard from her, and it was aimed at the prince.

The prince stared back at her. "I did not set the curse, my lady. Had I wanted, I have people for that. But you can blame neither them nor me." He seemed to consider his words. "It was a rather clever one, as curses go, though. Was it not?"

"Especially cruel. Unnecessarily so, if you ask me," Jules said.

He hummed. "And what price were you given to break it?"

Her look was level. "To marry one who was equal to my station."

They stared at each other for a very long moment.

Nickolas, meanwhile, continued in his confusion and gaping.

"And will you pay it?" the prince asked. "That price?"

Jules's voice was ice. "Not if the kingdom depended on it."

The prince gave a swift, decisive nod.

"Hold a moment." Nickolas barely recognized his own voice, let alone Jules's, as he held up a single finger to intercede. When the pair looked at him, he asked, "What the deuce is going on here?"

"A curse," Jules and the prince answered at once, and the prince twitched in irritation. He tapped a long finger to a button on his coat. The button looked, perhaps, to be crafted from solid gemstone. "A curse," the prince said again, his tone making clear he meant to own the pronouncement.

Nickolas glanced from one to the other. "Her or you?"

The prince said, "Both, it would seem. Though mine is the more pressing."

Jules scoffed.

The prince rolled his gaze skyward. "Let us be done with it."

And suddenly, without even a glimmer of warning, the room surrounding them disappeared.

NICKOLAS BLINKED, unsteady on ground that seemed to sway beneath his feet. Ground that was not the polished floor of the Filmore manor but greensward. He took a step backward and bumped against Jules.

She held the bird firmly against her chest, where he grumbled wildly inside a ruffled neck.

"You," Nickolas started. "You made a bargain. For that bird." *With a fae prince* seemed unnecessary to tack on, but he did so regardless.

The prince gave the pair of them a look. "I'll leave you to it," he said, waving a dismissive hand. To Jules, he added, "You know how to find me, should you change your mind."

"Never," she said again.

The prince's expression seemed to imply he was plagued by humans, then he was gone. As easily as he'd transported Nickolas, Jules, and the bird, the prince of Rivenwilde walked through the filigree wall.

Nickolas stared. The Rive, an ancient boundary that surrounded the kingdom, in place to prevent just such a fae from crossing, stood tall and imposing before them in the shape of a finely carved wall.

They were in the hollow heart of the forest. Nickolas had watched the prince walk through the filigree wall.

He stared longer, in wonder, at the sight he'd been granted by laying eyes on the prince. Part of the curse that kept the kingdoms safe had allowed Nickolas to see through fae glamour. The magic that had always hidden such things was suddenly revealed.

Nickolas did not like it. What had appeared as delicately chiseled stone was now writhing with forms in the shapes of man and beast, tangled wire and thorny vines caging them for all eternity. The two sights were layered overtop each other, human and fae, just like the creatures that appeared trapped within the stone. A stone hand reached forward, the barbed metal holding it back pierced through its chiseled forearm, while something vaguely wolflike clawed upward on its carved-stone hind legs, the thing's teeth bared and maw drawn in both directions by iron vine.

Nickolas suddenly yearned instead to be anywhere else, even penned inside Lord Carvell's courtyard.

"Lord Brigham," Jules said gently from beside him. "Perhaps we should go."

He turned on her. "Oh no, you don't. You did not just magically conduct us into the forest by fae bargain and then go on pretending all is well."

Frederick squawked.

"And you!" Nickolas said. "You can stay out of it. This is between me and my *wife*."

Jules slid a step back.

Nickolas advanced on her. "A curse. That was your secret? The trifling little thing you kept from me? *A fae curse?*"

She pressed her lips. "I never used the word *trifling*—"

"Indeed," he shot back. "You said naught of it at all. It's the most untrifling thing it could possibly be. What was it you called it? A minor legal matter? To break a betrothal. To a man of your station, apparently. But oh no, it was best that I find that out now from the *blasted* prince of the *blasted* fae."

"Nickolas, my lord, you seem a bit... overset."

"Over. Set. Truly?" He threw up his hands. "Yes. By all means, set me to rights." He pointed at her. "Tell me the terms of the curse."

She frowned.

"Right," he said. "None of that. Curse can't be spoken.

Can't ask for help. One of those, I'm sure." Saints, he couldn't believe it. He should have *known*. He was going to get back to the castle, back to... What had he been doing? Oh, right, he and his clandestine bride-to-be had just disappeared themselves in front of Nickolas's mother and two of her men. Though, to be fair, they'd had their backs turned and had not seen the prince. They might have no idea how he and Jules had escaped. "Etta," he said. "Etta can help us."

But for now, Nickolas realized, he needed to guess the curse. "Sleeping," he tried. "You're always sleeping."

Jules's expression went hard. "Is that a fault, Lord Brigham? Because you did not seem to mind earlier today."

When you dozed off and let your mother's men steal my bird, she meant.

He frowned, lifting his hand between them to wave off her remark. "Bad guess. I'll try again. Your face. It's not... Saints, of course not. How could it be real?"

She glared at him. "What does that mean?"

"Pardon me if it doesn't make sense that your..." His gaze fell from her expression to the way her fingers wrapped possessively around the bird. The bird that was glaring right along with her, dark eyes steely and judgmental. The breath seemed to rush from Nickolas's lungs. He stared at Jules accusingly. "It's... he's cursed. He's a cursed... there is a *person* inside of that bird. A *man*, to put a finer point on it."

"Nickolas," Jules said very carefully, "pray, do not faint inside this forest, as I'll not be able to drag you safely free of the trees."

He laughed, helpless and on edge. "Frederick. Frederick

is your..." The laughter trailed away as he looked at her. "Frederick is your..."

"Brother," she answered.

"Brother." He took a deep breath, maybe the first since he'd been thrown to the woods. Something echoed in the trees, bringing him back to his senses. They were in the forest, beside the filigree wall. Beyond it, upon a Riven throne, waited a prince and a curse. "Absolutely," he said in regard to no one in particular, "let us remove to the safety of the castle walls."

CHAPTER 10

It was nightfall before Nickolas and Jules came out of the forest. With his newly gifted sight, Nickolas experienced the altering of a world he had always considered fairly steady.

He had not taken the change well. With fae creatures shifting in every shadow, watching Jules and her bird with an intensity that put Frederick's glares to shame, Nickolas had, admittedly, handled it badly. It was to be expected. But after Jules had threatened to blindfold him and drag him back to the castle, Nickolas managed to pull himself together. He was not anticipating any particularly restful nights in his near future, though.

Nickolas and Jules stepped over the stones that marked the boundary, a warning that the edge of the forest was near, and something eased inside of him. "What about my mother's men?" he finally asked when they were near enough the castle walls that he felt as if his shoulders could dip beneath the level of his ears.

"I have a guard, and I am housed in the chancery. They

will not make an attempt on me there." She glanced up at him, and he nodded. "What of you? Will you be safe in your own rooms?"

"I've a lock on my door, so there's that. But breaking through locks is not typically how the lady Brigham operates. If she means to trap me, she will do so in plain sight."

"Then stay out of sight." Jules's voice was crisp.

"I am not certain how I will ever apologize for what she's done," he started.

Her gaze snapped to his again. "Do not. They were not your actions, and I refuse to hold you responsible."

He opened his mouth to argue, but her attention turned back to their path. "Besides, I knew full well what I was inviting upon myself by making a bargain with you."

"About that," Nickolas said.

She held up a hand. "There's Ian now."

The dark-haired man from their walk in the chancery gardens stood beside a castle outbuilding. He was dressed in neither livery nor finery, only a simple suit, sword at his hip and frown at the ready.

"Has he been watching the forest this entire time?" Nickolas asked.

"Doubtless he heard something was amiss. Or perhaps your carriage returned empty." She stopped and turned toward Nickolas.

She was leaving. Off with her man to the chancery. Something about the idea had him feeling bereft. "Frederick." He gestured toward the bird nestled against her chest. "He needs a cage. I could..." Saints protect him. "Would you like me to pick one up for him at the aviary?"

The bird gave Nickolas a dark look.

"Thank you," Jules said. "But Ian can manage it."

They stood for a moment longer. In his nondescript suit by his nondescript block wall, Ian straightened.

"Right." Nickolas bowed his head. "Good night, my lady."

"Good night, Lord Brigham."

THE FIRST THING Nickolas had done upon returning to his rooms was lock his door. But shortly afterward, he'd written a note for Etta. Nickolas might have been rattled by his encounter with the prince, but though it was the first time he'd witnessed a fae, it was not the first time he'd witnessed foul magic. He understood Jules was in trouble. She had made a bargain with Nickolas because a curse had been laid upon her.

He had to help her break it.

And so, early the next morning, he was in the office of the marshal of Westrende. "Truly," he said, standing in the center of a room that felt palatial and fighting the desire to make a slow spin, head tilted back to take it in. "All this for a marshal?"

The lady Ostwind gave him a level stare from where she sat behind her massive desk. "I'm the head of law and order for the entire kingdom, Nickolas. What did you expect?"

He shook his head. "A bit of modesty, I suppose. Could have at least tried putting some on."

She leaned forward. "I have work to do. Perhaps you could muster sufficient nerve to tell me whatever it is you're avoiding"—her finger tapped irritably on a stack of correspondence atop her desk—"and what it has to do with a late-night order that I send a half-dozen kingsmen to stand watch outside the chancery sleeping quarters."

The chagrin that crossed his face was not put on. "*Order* is a strong word."

Etta shuffled through the stack, drawing out a single page. "... and therefore demand no less than fifteen armed men at all times posted as noted at each of the following locations throughout the chancery—"

"All right. I was under duress. I'd just had a shock." Nickolas bit his lip. "You did send them, did you not?"

She sighed. "I did."

He nodded. "Thank you. That means a great deal."

"And the shock?"

"Right." He settled heavily into the chair that sat opposite her desk. "I saw the prince."

"The prince." Her voice changed, gone as steady as a general. If there was a being who possessed all of the ire inside of Antonetta Ostwind, it was the prince of the Riven Court.

Nickolas leaned back to run a hand over his face. "Yes. That one." Etta was very quiet, and when he finally looked at her again, he found her expression was as deadly as a general as well.

He owed her an apology, he knew. Etta had the sight. She had seen the prince when she'd been only a girl.

Nickolas had not believed her. Like everyone else, he'd thought Westrende was safe from the fae. "It was horrendous," he said.

"Lady Brigham's men have been sniffing around the

chancery. You've asked that guards be placed there. Outside of Jules's rooms," she said.

A long breath fell from his lungs.

Etta nodded slowly. She hadn't earned her position by being a fool. "At your warning, Gideon set his own kingsmen to watch. The chancery will be the safest place for her." She leaned forward, not softly as she might have done as his friend but sharply, the posture of a marshal of Westrende. "What has this to do with your mother?"

Nickolas held back the wild sob that wanted to escape. What came out instead was sort of a helpless laugh. "Nothing at all. She merely wishes me to marry Lady Carvell." To restore the family name.

"Who laid eyes on the prince? Who else has the sight?"

"My mother and her ruffians were turned away. So only me and Jules. But she... Well, Jules has evidently already met him."

"Because of a curse."

Nickolas slid a hand over the fabric covering his knee. "She can't tell me. Each time she starts to speak of it, her words choke off." Or she grabbed at whatever hung from a chain at her neck, he thought. "It's that ridiculous bird of hers. That's part of the curse. Her brother, she says. He's trapped inside the creature. Hates me, by the way. Doesn't spare a chance to let me know it."

He threw up a hand. "And I don't know what it means, how any of it is tied to her curse, or how to stop it. I'm only certain it must have been laid on her ages ago and that the prince and she were aware of one another before being in each other's company yesterday. She needed to get out of a betrothal, so she bargained with me to gain access to places she could not go on her own. Introductions, you know. She wanted to break the curse. And she kept saying..." She had kept saying it would be over soon. He looked up at Etta. "Her time must be almost up."

"The full moon," Etta said. "It's always ending on a full moon with this sort, fae rituals and all. Well, that explains why she's working in the chancery office." At Nickolas's blank look, Etta explained, "To learn the laws of the kingdom so she can unhitch herself from... this other man, whoever he is."

"Laws," Nickolas said. "*Books.*"

Etta's gaze narrowed on him. "Do you need a moment to gather your thoughts? Perhaps before you speak?"

He shook his head. "The library. We were at the Filmore library because she needed to find a book." He went still at her reaction. "What?"

"What?" Etta parroted back.

"You tell me what." He pointed at her. "You've got that look. The one you get when you know something you don't plan to tell me. There! That one. Give it up, Antonetta. This isn't a game."

"I know it's not, you dolt. It's precisely the sort of foolery you should not be messing about with. This is serious kingdom business."

Nickolas leaned forward. "Oh no you don't. I'm in this, just like last time, and you're not going to keep me in the dark until I end up—"

"It was *one* time," Etta snapped. "I got you into trouble *one* time."

"Jail, Antonetta. You got me into *jail.*"

Her lips pressed down. "I may know the book. There was a certain collection of fae laws my father had." At his attempt at rising, she held up a hand as if to stall him. "It's no longer in our possession. Gideon has moved it some-where safe."

"Can it help her? Does it hold whatever clues she needs to break a curse?"

Etta looked doubtful. "Not without knowing the terms she's bound by. What about the other favor, the intro-duction?"

"She's asked to meet with Lord Beckett."

Etta hummed. "Beckett specializes in interkingdom law. Perhaps the threat of a betrothal at home is why she's hiding in Westrende, looking for asylum. But it's no wonder she could not ask Gideon to assist her in an intro-duction to Beckett. The man has ties to his uncle."

"The steward?"

She nodded. "The very one."

Nickolas leaned back in his chair. Jules had said she did not want to put Gideon and Etta at risk. He'd not under-stood precisely how real that danger was. Fae curses and kingdom officials could not mix. He shook his head. "Well, at least that part, I have covered. I plan to introduce her to Beckett at the midsummer ball."

Etta stared at him. After a moment, she asked, "You're taking her to a ball?"

Nickolas stood abruptly. "I'm helping her. That's all." It was all, truly. She was just a lady who was cursed, and he was taking her to a ball. Etta's eyes still on him, he said defensively, "Find the book. I'll do the rest." Then he turned and walked out the door.

CHAPTER 11

Nickolas strode into the wide corridor outside Etta's office just as kingdom business came into full swing. Lords and ladies, kingsmen, officials, and sundry messengers, staff, and scribes filled the imposing space. Nickolas had a list of those lords he was meant to meet with. He needed to review his proposal for the next assembly and, most unfortunately, had run out of excuses not to stop at the exchequer's office to handle some delicate Brigham family business. He would do so today.

"Nicky."

A hand smacked overhard onto Nickolas's shoulder along with the overloud voice. He held back the expression that wanted to claw its way across his face. Lords did not reveal unpleasant tempers in the council's wing of the castle. "William," he said without breaking his stride.

The other man rushed to keep up, not letting go his grip. "Still churlish, I see. Word about Westrende is that you have a new lady on your arm. Giving you trouble, is she?"

Nickolas stopped and turned so abruptly that a scribe knocked into William from behind when he stopped too. "Remove your hand from my person, Lord Adair."

William stepped back. "I see how it is, then."

Something heavy settled in Nickolas's gut. Would that it was only guilt.

William's head tipped closer at his reaction. "Remembering my connections, I see, that a word from me could do more damage than even a Brigham's reputation might bear." His voice had gone smooth, no longer the brash boy he so often pretended to be.

Nickolas said nothing and merely let the cold steadiness of his expression do its work.

The other man's tone dipped in its cajoling. "Come, Nickolas. Our families have been friends for years. I just need a moment of your time. That's all."

Nickolas asked, "What is it that you want, Will?"

His sharp green eyes darted from one direction of the corridor to another. He wore a superfine coat of a shade darker than his eyes, his muddy-hued side-whiskers dipping beneath his shirt points in a pale imitation of his father's. He truly was a menace. "Just a moment of privacy."

Nickolas gave a nod of acquiescence and followed the man to a private meeting room farther down the corridor. Once inside, Nickolas moved away from the darkened alcove, where William latched the door.

Unease crawled up Nickolas's neck, and he couldn't help but snap, "What is it?"

William clicked his tongue. "So that's how it will be, then? Even among old friends?"

"I wasn't under the impression this was a friendly interview, Lord Adair. It smacks of distrain."

A dark chuckle came from behind Nickolas as William moved to face him. "Very well. We'll get to the point. I need something from you, Lord Brigham."

That was nothing new. "I've naught left to give, and you know it."

William's wide mouth slid into an unpleasant grin. "I do. But you have one asset left, do you not? And I intend to use it. You, my fine friend, will do precisely as I ask, or the Brigham name will be turned to muck. No one with a single tie to your family will be spared, least of all your lady mother."

The truth in the threat was plain. The Adairs had information on Nickolas's mother. They'd used it for years to siphon obligations from Nickolas's father. But Nickolas's father was gone.

"Why now? What reason could you possibly have?" Nickolas asked.

The eldest of a long line of Adair heirs leaned a hip against the table and crossed his arms. "Princess Mireille."

Nickolas stared dumbly. "What about her? The woman is three kingdoms away."

"She's coming to the ball. Word is she means to find a husband and strengthen ties with Westrende. I intend to win her."

"Win her? Saints, what are you—" Nickolas's words cut off when he realized what William was planning. The lady was worth a small fortune on her own. But if one could win the support of the lady's father and influence trade from the inside... Nickolas leaned heavily against the nearby wall.

"All I need is a post. To look as if the thing hasn't been set up. A valid title so that, by appearance, I've a different goal. And you, my friend"—a long finger pointed menacingly at Nickolas—"you will get me that spot. Something impressive at the hands of your bosom confidant. And don't tell me the two of you have fallen out. I just saw you leave her."

"You expect a post in the marshal's office?" Nickolas asked, his tone incredulous. "Ostwind would tear you apart."

Will leaned forward. "Let me worry about that."

"It will never work. You have to see that."

William rose to his full height. "You seem to believe this is a favor I'm asking, Lord Brigham. Be assured, it is not. You will secure me a post in the office of marshal by the end of the week, or your four sisters will pay the price."

He dropped a coin onto the table then strode from the room. Nickolas could hear the horrible man's whistle fade into the distance as if he'd not just tossed a threat to the entire Brigham family onto the fine wood table.

Nickolas's mother had never been satisfied. Despite the riches her status provided—the comfort, the security, a lavish lifestyle, and societal respect—there was never enough. Tempted by riffraff, she'd found ways to feed that dissatisfaction. Minor offenses at first, smuggled goods that were not entirely legal, dishonest trades with neighboring kingdoms. But she'd gotten greedy. She became involved with a group who dabbled in more illicit crimes, like forgery. Nickolas's father had chased her debts, ensuring her safety but emptying the coffers even before his death.

The squandering had not stopped. Lady Brigham had

driven the family into insolvency beyond repair. She'd betrayed their name for the endless desire for more. And the coin was carved with a reminder of those crimes.

Nickolas stared at it, understanding exactly how dangerous his mother's secret was in the hands of William Adair and unable to stop it.

CHAPTER 12

Nickolas had not laid eyes on Jules since the day she had left him outside of the castle. He'd been thwarted first by his mother's men sniffing around the chancery then again when he'd arrived to find Gideon at odds with some lord who was part of Princess Mireille's entourage attempting to force access to the wing. The risk of being spotted and Nickolas's failed attempts to visit personally had led him to send a message to Jules, which was followed only by a brief conversation with her through a thin panel in a nearby document room.

Ian had stood watch as Nickolas leaned close to the panel, whispering assurances that the masked ball would be Jules's best chance at an introduction to Lord Beckett. "We will find him, and we will sort your troubles. Soon, this will all be only a dark spot in your past."

"I hear your words, Lord Brigham, but I fear they do not ring true. Time is running out for me, and I'm afraid new complications have arisen."

His finger had lifted to trace the thin grooves in the

panel that made up a larger pattern of decorative vines. "My lady, let us try."

There was a long moment of stillness. When her voice came again, it was closer, as if she had pressed near the panel on her own side. "We will try," she said. "For it is all there is to do."

Her tone made it evident that she'd given up hope. For his part, Nickolas had not sought out his mother, had not attempted to convince Antonetta that his extortionist associate should be given a post in the marshal's office, and was very much feeling the same sort of resigned despair that he sensed in Jules.

The Brighams would be ruined, come one thing or another. Tying himself to a Carvell or playing into a scheme of the Adairs would only make it worse. Perhaps he should renounce his title and move to the country to take up gardening, or a trade for which he had no skill at all, until their creditors came calling. Perhaps he might strip off his clothes and dance atop the courtyard wall to have it all done with faster.

"You look quite fine," he said dourly to his reflection. "Even if it may be the last time you'll dress in velvet and gilt trim." He'd chosen his finest black coat to wear over the stiff white shirt, with black pants and black shoes. His mask was sleek and dark, shaped to cover him from nose to brow. The only spot of color would be Jules on his arm.

He strode from his suite and toward the grand ballroom, every part of the castle alive with bustle and conversation that only grew as he neared the hall. So much anticipation surrounded the event, and delight at its secrets and masks, that Nickolas had no trouble slipping through unnoticed. He was slowed only when an older man bumped into him, as the man was jostled by the crowd that was gathered where the princess awaited entry. Lords and ladies clamored to catch a glimpse of her court, making the corridor overhot and heavily scented by perfumes.

He steadied the man then adjusted course to walk closer to the wall, weaving around statuary and a man in a deep-blue coat. Nickolas recognized him as the lord who'd attempted access to the chancery. The man had the look of a guard, gaze sharp as it traversed the crowd, and Nickolas wondered how many of Mireille's entourage were not mere courtiers. Surely William was not the only person who had eyes on interkingdom relations, trade or otherwise.

The doors to the ballroom opened, finally allowing the milling guests to go inside, and Nickolas's way became clearer. He glanced over his shoulder before releasing the lever to a small room adjacent to the corridor, where he was to meet Jules. Across the crowded space, the chancellor of Westrende watched from his place beside a pillar. Nickolas could not help the smirk that tipped the edge of his lips upward, as Gideon might be masked and attired in something other than his customary uniform coat, but Nickolas would recognize that stuffy posture anywhere.

Gideon frowned.

The latch clicked open, and Nickolas stepped inside.

Across the space was the familiar figure he'd encountered for the first time only days before in a midnight garden. Everything else in the room fell away. Jules was radiant. Lady Roth had outdone herself with a fine silk gown in the palest shade of blue and topped with a sheer layer dotted with embroidery and jewels. The bodice was trimmed with a delicate strip of lace, cut lower than Jules's usual gowns to reveal a single ring hanging from the end of the familiar golden chain. Her arms were bare above a pair of long white gloves, smooth skin luminous in the candlelight. In the corner of the room, Ian cleared his throat.

Nickolas swallowed hard. His gaze rose to Jules's face. "My lady," he said with his grandest bow, "you are exquisite."

Jules's mouth was in a strange line, her brow knit beneath a delicate mask of white and blue and not a single feather on her person, thank the fates and Lady Roth.

"Lord Brigham," she said.

He stepped closer, unable to prevent the flash of his smile when he added "Enchanting" with a closer look at her mask. Saints, her eyes were wild and dangerous things.

"And you," she said, though he wasn't certain the words were a compliment, given her consternation.

He lifted a gloved hand to take hers. He held it for a moment too long. They both knew it. He said, "Thank you, my lady, for not bringing along your bird."

Her dark eyes narrowed.

"I trust your man has something to occupy him while we are gone."

Jules glanced at Ian. "Oh, he will be attending with us."

"Not *with* us," Nickolas said.

The man's only reply was a speaking glance. The words it spoke were something like *I know well how to perform my duties*, and *I will be watching you precisely as much as I dislike you, which is entirely*.

Nickolas gave him a friendly smile. "Splendid. Happy to have you along. At a substantial distance." Nickolas turned his smile on Jules, who seemed slightly nonplussed. He'd had that effect on women before. He released his charm with full vigor, leaning closer as he moved to her side, and she appeared to force her gaze away. Keeping hold of her hand to press it over his arm, he said, "Come now. The ball awaits."

Jules's evident trepidation did not ease as they entered the ballroom. She held herself stiff, seemingly unmoved by the lights and the music or the midsummer decorations scattered throughout the lavish space. Her gaze stayed on the crowd, as if scanning faces in spite of the masks. Nickolas wondered if she was anxious to see someone in particular. "Shall we attempt to catch a glimpse of the royal Norcliffe party?"

"No," she gasped. "That would be the worst possible thing."

Nickolas had been raised attending Westrende events, and even he found himself dazzled by the grandness of their special occasions from time to time. Perhaps he'd misunderstood her mood and she was uncomfortable. He dipped his head to whisper in her ear, "Would you prefer to leave, my lady?"

A shiver seemed to roll through her, and she drew back to look up at him. He had the sensation of seeing her for the first time, but he was not unaware that every eye in the room was on them. Like Gideon, Nickolas was not a figure a simple mask could disguise.

"No," Jules said determinedly. "We must meet with Lord Beckett."

Nickolas nodded toward the far wall, angling Jules for a

better view by gentle pressure on their connected arms. She had not, thus far, let go of him. "That is Lord Beckett there. The tall, handsome fellow in the impeccable black coat. Dark skin, white pants, standing beside the lady in the yellow gown who seems to—saints, yes, that is a half yard of dyed feathers protruding from her wig. Best not to let these ladies near your Frederick. They'd have him plucked and bare before you could say *quill*. Just there, see. Can't miss it."

Jules's gaze no more than landed on Lord Beckett before she started toward the man.

Nickolas held her arm. "My lady, the queue surrounding Beckett looks hours long. Let us enjoy the festivities while we wait for a more opportune moment."

She glanced at him, the mask slipping down a fraction with her brow.

Nickolas reached up to tip it back into place. "I promise, love, you will have your chance at him, even if I have to battle every lord in this room to see it done." He rested his free hand on the hilt of his sword. "But let us take the more decorous route if we can."

"What are we to do for those hours?"

He straightened, humor dancing at the edge of his lips once more. "At a ball? The fates only know. Dreadfully boring things. Everyone says so." When she did not answer, he leaned closer. Nothing was worse than being pressured into something one did not enjoy or had no confidence in before a room full of judgmental peers. But he could not stand to *not* ask her. "How do you feel about dancing, my lady?"

The look she gave him was one of surprise, and she seemed to consider, then to decide she'd nothing else to occupy her wait, before offering her hand. "I suppose that would do well enough."

"Such a flatterer, you. Swooning at my every attention. I'm not certain how much more of this my dignity can take."

"I suspect your pride can bear it," she said as he led her to the dance floor.

He pressed a hand to his heart. "You wound me." The orchestra was without fault, renowned even kingdoms away, and their symphony swelled just as Nickolas turned to face her. He bowed. She dipped into a curtsy, and they fell into step with the teeming crowd around them.

Jules was a better dancer than he was. Far superior, despite all his training. Saints, she moved like a... well, like nothing he'd ever seen. Her chin was up, eyes forward, flawless form revealing not a hint of concern for the courtiers who might be watching. They would certainly be watching, he remembered, so he forced his gaze away from his partner to perform the dance. Rue throbbed sharp inside his chest, but he ignored it. Jules was betrothed, to someone truly awful from whom she had to escape. He did not know how to help her, and each step of the dance that turned him to face her, each time the light caught on the chain about her slender neck, felt like another plunge of the knife.

The music ended, and they danced again, and because the rules of propriety slackened at a masquerade, Nickolas led them into a third. When it was over, he took her hand, bowing so low before her that he might have kissed it. But he only returned to standing, stealing no more than the slide of his thumb across the back of her hand before letting go.

"What now?" he asked, feeling slightly breathless. It must have been deuced warm in the ballroom. "The refreshment table? Rumor has it there's to be a lavish display of sugared fruit this year and an endless supply of cakes."

When she merely replied, "If you'd like," he led her to the side of the room.

"Perhaps you'll sneak some back for Frederick. Though he likely prefers seeds and grain."

"Bread," she said. When Nickolas glanced at her, she repeated, "I give him bread."

Nickolas stared down at her, her eyes serious beneath the fine mask, her lashes long and dark. He felt himself shift closer, and when Jules's mouth parted, his ears pricked in anticipation of whatever she meant to say.

Then the flock of ladies browsing the dessert table descended and he straightened, increasing the distance between him and Jules. It was poor timing, to say the least.

The ladies fawned and fluttered while Nickolas did his best to politely disengage. He made no formal introduction because Jules was to remain unknown, but when a lady who was the cousin to the stablemaster pressed, "You must, if nothing else, tell us how you met," Jules replied for him, the hint of a smile flirting with the edge of her lips.

"Lord Brigham fell into my courtyard." She glanced up at him adoringly. "Like a little baby bird shoved from its nest too soon."

The hem of rebuke in his throat was drowned out by tittering ladies. Annoyed, Nickolas slid an arm possessively around Jules, his gaze on their audience. "If you'll allow me to make my excuses, ladies, I have made promises of cake that I intend to keep."

Once the others were gone and Jules was reaching for a small plate that held a pair of delicate treats, Nickolas leaned in, voice low in the hope of regaining their moment before the interruption. "My apologies. Some days, society simply cannot get enough of my conversation."

She made a snort of incredulity. "I'm surprised you allow yourself such a credit. They seemed not at all concerned with a word that fell from your mouth. Indeed, Lord Brigham, I fear they were trifling with you. If they'd not been busy perusing you in your fine suit, in the way they perused the dessert table, you wouldn't get half so far or even a quarter with most courtiers."

A startled laugh came out of him. "So you *do* believe me handsome."

She bit into a cookie.

"Or delicious, like the desserts," he said. "I'll admit, I suspected as much from the start. 'That Jules,' I said, 'she cannot take her eyes from me.' Like a lodestone, I am. It's a burden, truly, to hold this sort of power over a lady. I worry myself about it day and night."

She dropped her half-eaten ginger cookie to the plate meaningfully.

He pressed his lips together in surrender then offered her a glass of punch.

The moment was gone, but they made a tour of the room, taking in the fine decorations and elegant dress. Nickolas told Jules of some of the oldest Westrende traditions and ushered her to view a particularly stunning landscape, then they made their way to a pair of doors that led out into a courtyard. The space was cool and moonlit, a few flickering candelabra placed around the entrance to the ballroom. The scene reminded him of the night he'd met her. "A baby bird," he muttered as he recalled what she'd said about him falling into her life.

Her expression was solemn with not a twitch of the lip when she looked up at him. "Indeed. Helpless and lost. Poor creature."

Trapped in a cage, he thought, unable to climb the walls Carvell and his mother had built around him. The expectation. The debt. He'd failed to get free, and yet, even now, it was as if Jules was saving him from facing those gallows. He let out a breath, and if it fell across the bare skin above her neckline, he could not be blamed for it. "How fortunate for me that you have a soft spot for pitiable creatures." Music rose from inside the hall, and he had the intense desire to take her into his arms once more. "Dance with me, my lady. Before our time is over."

She took a step closer, dark eyes shining beneath her mask. He suspected she'd heard the lament in his tone, but instead of addressing it, she asked, "And how have you found this evening, my lord?"

He gave Jules a self-deprecating smile as she lifted a hand to take his. They spun gently over the flat stones that bordered the courtyard. Beyond them, masked couples paraded past, gracing the pair with fond smiles and whispering quietly of things best said in moonlit gardens. "Dreadfully dull," Nickolas murmured as Jules twirled in a step that brought her back to him. "Never had such a tedious night of dancing and discussion in my life. And the company..." He shook his head. "This will be the memory I draw forth when I need to appear as if I'm taking an assembly presentation seriously."

Jules laughed, the sound light and musical and carefree.

His heart danced. He wanted to hear it again. He wanted to make her laugh and to—

He froze. The foolish grin that had somehow found its way to his face dropped like a stone in his stomach.

"What's the matter?" she whispered, her steps coming to a halt. "What happened?"

"I—" He shook his head, loosening his grip on her. "Nothing. It's nothing." He swallowed and took a short step back from her. His hand flexed at his waist, palm still warm from the heat of her, wanting to reclaim its grasp. "Perhaps we should—that is, I'm afraid I may no longer be able to—" He cleared his throat, strengthened his resolve. "I've just recalled another engagement, my lady. Our evening must end here. I regret if I have misled you in any way, but this—"

"There you are." The voice came from the open doorway to the ballroom, slicing through whatever words Nickolas might have said.

Off his guard entirely, he glanced toward the voice, startled to recognize a lord he'd met years before. The lord had been a visiting envoy from Norcliffe. Nickolas straightened automatically before dipping swiftly into a low bow. He felt Jules's hesitation beside him, then came relief when she fell into a curtsy. They both rose, Jules keeping her head bowed, eyes downcast. She had not been introduced, and before them, fate save them, stood the princess of Norcliffe and several members of her court.

The familiar lord came forward. "Lord Brigham. I've been searching for you. You must be introduced to her highness. She's been eager to finally meet you."

The princess stepped gracefully from among the crowd of courtiers, thin silver mask covering only her eyes, embroidered gown trimmed exceptionally well in gold. She was tall and dignified, her manner seeming more affable than prim. Nickolas had not expected her to be so striking. William would have to use every tool and trick at his disposal to win a woman of her status.

Her Highness, Princess Mireille, may I present—"

"Lord Brigham," the princess interrupted smoothly. "Please, let us not stand on ceremony. I feel as if I know you so well by the stories our mutual friends have imparted." Her lips tilted playfully. "You have quite the reputation for misadventure, my lord."

"All lies, I assure you." A crowd had gathered around the doorway, both inside and out of the ballroom. Nickolas inclined his head. "Highness. It is a privilege." Out of the corner of his vision, Nickolas saw Ian moving across the courtyard but could not take his gaze off the courtiers, the elder Lord Adair and his sons among them, and Lord Carvell with his daughter. Nickolas's skin prickled at the nape.

He shifted to introduce Jules, but she no longer stood at his side. She was gone. He cleared his throat.

Princess Mireille reached forward, taking Nickolas's arm. "Come," she said. "Let us stroll through the courtyard. Perhaps you will tell me stories and, afterward, invite me to dance."

Nickolas glanced over his shoulder, searching, but found no sign of Jules. Ian was evidently gone as well, the figures that had been milling about the courtyard now closing in. "I'm afraid I..." He tilted his head for a better look past the moonlit topiary and saw a slip of delicate silvery blue disappear into a far-off doorway before a pair of figures blocked his view.

The princess slid her hand companionably into the crook of Nickolas's arm. "Call me Rei, please."

Nickolas's gaze returned to hers. Saints, up close she was even lovelier. Her features were fine, dark-olive skin glowing in the torchlight, her scent light and flowery instead of the heavier perfumes so many peers wore. She was waiting for him. He knew it. The crowd was waiting for him too. He was meant to take her through the courtyards, to charm her and try to win her with the games courtiers played. He was a Brigham. It was practically his duty.

But he didn't know what had happened to Jules. He glanced once more through the courtyard, finding the lord he'd seen arguing with Gideon outside of the chancery only days before now speaking with Carvell. Nickolas didn't like leaving Jules unattended. His mother's men might be anywhere nearby. At the very least, he should apologize. He should escort her back to her rooms.

The princess gave a gentle squeeze to Nickolas's arm.

"I'm sorry, Highness, but... I must go." He withdrew his arm from hers, to the stunned gasps of the onlookers, and gave a cursory bow. "If you'll forgive me."

Her expression revealed surprise, but she inclined her head courteously.

He stepped forward once more and leaned in to tell her quietly, "Be wary, Your Highness, of suitors with interest in trade." At the edge of the doorway, inside the ballroom, Nickolas caught sight of Lady Brigham's deadly glare. He swore silently, and the moment she was swallowed up by the shifting crowd, he turned to move hastily away.

CHAPTER 13

Nickolas sped through the courtyard, keeping himself hidden from view of the ballroom as best he could. Ornamental shrubs rose around him in tall cones, and the pathway was edged in wisteria, sweet and musky in the still night air. The muffled voices and distant echo of the orchestra faded, replaced by the hollow babble of fountains.

It took three tries to find the door through which Jules had disappeared, and when he finally did, he was only certain it was the right one because the moment he opened it, a hulking man slammed into him and rolled him to the ground. Sword still sheathed—they'd been in a courtyard outside a ballroom, for fate's sake—Nickolas wrapped his hands around the man's coat sleeves and jerked him to the side. The man was stout; he barely moved at all.

Nickolas wedged his elbows between himself and the man's chest and twisted, gaining enough space to free one of his legs. But he was no more than half liberated before he was flat on his back again. Long limbs his only advantage, he slipped an arm over the man's shoulder, wrapped it about his thick head, and pulled in a spin. The man flattened his feet to the ground for leverage, at one point calling Nickolas a beef-witted bamboozler and spitting a bit of what was probably blood—Nickolas was no novice, despite the other man's superior size—before they were rolling again. Finally gaining the upper hand, Nickolas tried to shove away, but formal shoes weren't meant for scuffling, and he slipped in the slime and shattered remnants of a clay pot the pair had knocked to the floor.

Off balance, Nickolas was an easy target, and the man leapt, as quick as a bull, to pin him to the ground once more.

Nickolas drew his fist back, entirely spent of gentlemanly restraint, then froze when a bucket of tepid, reeking plant-water was thrown onto both of them.

Nickolas blinked up to find Jules standing over them, her expression oddly vacant. She let go of the bucket, and it clanged to the floor beside them. When she turned away, Nickolas shoved the man's forearm off his chest with a grunt of disgust. Ian—for Nickolas was finally certain, in the sparse light coming through the room's windows, that that was who his opponent had been—slid to the side, running a hand over his close-cropped hair and flicking the water free.

Jules stepped away then turned and leaned against a long gardening table to remove her soiled gloves. "The two of you are done now."

Wet and thoroughly reprimanded, Nickolas and Ian sat in repentant silence, their chests heaving for breath. Nickolas did not argue that he was not responsible, that *he'd* been the one attacked. Not since he understood what Ian's job was. Nickolas had never seen a man fight in that manner. Ian was meant to be Jules's protector; he might have jumped on anyone who came through the door. "Saints. Where did you train to be a guard? You're deuced awful at it."

The man looked up at him. "I'm not a guard, you daft cad." He ran a thumb over the split on his lip. "I'm her coachman."

"Her..." Nickolas glanced at Jules. Whatever question he'd meant to ask shriveled at the sight of her. It appeared she was, to put it mildly, unsettled. He pushed to his feet, not bothering to brush off the soil and muck he and Ian had rolled in. Something was wrong. "My lady, what is it?"

She shook her head, the distress he'd seen in her expression tinged with grief.

"You can't tell me?" he asked. "Because of the curse."

She nodded.

Nickolas glanced at—well, at her coachman, evidently.

"Ian doesn't know," she said. "He can't give you the details any more than I can."

The man sighed then gathered himself to his feet. "I only know what I saw."

"What did you see?"

He gave Nickolas his full gaze. "That something very bad happened. And she needed my protection."

"Was it the prince of the Riven Court? Did you see him? You would have known—been given the sight."

"Doesn't work like that where we come from. That bird she carries around isn't dressed up to look like a bird. He *is* a bird. Laying eyes on our fae doesn't win you a thing. That's your kingdom's curse, not ours."

"Hold a moment," Nickolas said. "What kingdom is yours, specifically?"

The man's mouth went into a flat line, and Nickolas let out a long breath. "Right. So, she cannot tell me, and you're unwilling. You'll only say that something bad happened, that she needed protection, and..."

At Nickolas's prompt, Ian added, "And I went after her. Whatever it is, whatever was done, I know she had reason. I trust her."

Nickolas's gaze slid to Jules. Her eyes were on him, but her cheeks had gone hot. Ian had said more than she'd meant to have revealed. "Someone is after you," Nickolas guessed. And not just her family to tie her to a betrothal. She'd been accused of a misdeed, some sort of serious offense, so she'd fled to Westrende. "And that someone is from your own kingdom."

There was a muffled scraping sound in the courtyard, and they all glanced toward the narrow window that bordered the door.

The man from Princess Mireille's court—the one who'd been arguing with Gideon outside of the chancery—peered back at them through the thick glass.

Ian stood with a curse, and when Nickolas moved with him, Ian said, "No, stay with her. I'll catch the rotter."

Jules had shrunk back, and Nickolas moved toward her, eyes on the closed door through which Ian had disappeared. "Who was that?"

With no real spirit, she swatted a glove at him, so he turned to face her. "The man I was *hiding* from." Then she burst into tears. Or at least the impression of such. It was a sort of dry, soundless sob, all emotion and none of the wet, unpleasant fluids or noise.

It did not make the whole thing less terrible. In fact, it somehow made it worse. It was like another dagger in his heart—how many was that now, seven? "Jules," he said softly, wrapping his arms around her where she struggled to draw breath. It was not merely a bit of distress. Hers were the motions of pure grief.

Hiding, she'd said. "Why? Because he was from Norcliffe? Is that your home?"

She shook her head, not, he gathered, to indicate it was or was not the kingdom from which she'd escaped but rather that she could not tell him more.

"And I have brought you to him, paraded you at a ball where any one of them might put you in harm's way." He ran a hand lightly over her back. "What if Ian finds the man? Will that sort it?"

She shook her head against his chest. She'd already said she could not involve Gideon, which meant whatever she'd done was serious enough they would be law-bound to send her back.

He slid one hand up to cradle the back of her neck. It was warm and soft, and so was his voice. "Then we will find a way to hide you."

She drew away to look up at him, her face soft in the moonlight, her nose tipped with pink.

He ran a thumb over her cheek. "Does that sound agreeable?"

"They will come for me. It won't matter about the..." Her fingers curled around the ring that hung from her neck as if its chain were choking her.

He placed his hand over hers. "You're afraid they will return you home and you'll be forced to marry, or is it something else? How much trouble are you up against, my lady?"

She swallowed. "They won't force me to marry any man. They'll force me to—he'll be—" Her words choked off again, and she shook her head. "You can't understand. I cannot explain it."

"My lady, it does not matter. Whatever it is, we will face it together. That was our bargain."

Her shoulders eased in his embrace, and her lips parted to speak. But the door to the room slammed open.

Nickolas's gaze shot toward the sound. Just in time, it turned out, to watch Lady Brigham storm in. Behind her, a handful of courtiers and castle staff looked on from the courtyard. She posted herself before the entrance, almost militant in her posture, and faced Nickolas and Jules. Her intent was clear—to punish Nickolas and hurt anyone who held his concern. Nothing particularly new, but Nickolas had met his limit.

"Oh, for the love of—" He stepped out of the embrace to turn on his mother. "Enough." The word split into two, possibly three. He'd never been so angry in his life. "This is it, Mother. I am done. I have tried. I have done my utmost to save this family and preserve our name. But no more." He glared her down. "The Brighams do not *deserve* to be saved."

His mother took a step toward him.

Nickolas turned to the crowd of onlookers who'd gathered outside the open door. "We're cleaned out," he told them. "Done for. Pockets to let, rolled-up, on the rocks. The Brighams have no funds." At the intake of breath from a lady he thought was employed in the kitchens, Nickolas added, "It gets worse. It's not merely destitution. I'm afraid there are unspeakably dishonorable acts to add to the—"

His confession was cut short by the shriek that came from his mother. The entire courtyard went silent, making not a sound aside from the echo of babbling water.

His mother's eyes cut to Jules, and her hand balled into a fist. "Taking up with a clerk's assistant in a dark garden shed at the midsummer ball and you have the nerve to speak to me of dishonorable acts."

Nickolas remembered, quite suddenly, that Jules had been wrapped in his arms when his mother had entered. He resisted the urge to tell the crowd that it was not what it looked like. He edged in front of Jules. "This is not the time, Mother. In fact, it will never be the time again. We are done. It is over. And it's nothing to do with Jules."

"You gave up our chance at a princess. She was practically begging to drag us from the edge of ignobility."

Nickolas felt his brow draw down. He hadn't even considered making suit for the princess. He'd only needed to check on Jules.

When his mother demanded, "Go after her *now*. Tell Mireille you've changed your mind," Nickolas found he could not move.

His mother's air became more dangerous. "I didn't want to do this, but you've given me no choice."

Nickolas did not like her tone. When she spoke again, he knew his impression was right.

His mother, the distinguished Lady Brigham of the renowned Brigham line, committed a crime so heinous no law had even been written to cover it.

She spoke the fae prince's name.

"Have you lost your senses entirely?" Nickolas heard himself shout.

His mother had, evidently, because she did not even shy away as the fae prince materialized in the corner of the room. She must have somehow seen the prince at the Filmore estate, or perhaps not. Perhaps she'd only heard Jules whisper his name. But it was clear her action was planned. Nickolas swore.

The fae prince took a look at his surroundings, made an unpleasant face, then stepped from the shadows. He inclined his head to Jules. "My lady."

At his back, Nickolas could feel Jules nod in return.

The prince's gaze trailed briefly over the watching crowd, at least three of whom had fainted, then landed on Lady Brigham. She stood straight and formal as if waiting for an introduction to be made.

Etta was going to kill Nickolas. He would need to make record of everyone standing within view to report to the marshal's office so that she could deal with whatever followed. The paperwork *alone*. What a nightmare. Perhaps he should have danced naked through the courtyard after all and been thrown into the dungeon where he belonged.

"Nickolas," his mother snapped.

"What? You called him. You want to stand on propriety *now*?" At her glare, he turned toward the prince. "May I introduce Lady Brigham, Your Highness?" He gestured vaguely in her direction before grandly rolling his hand toward the prince. "Mother, the prince of Rivenwilde."

The prince's gaze slid from Nickolas to his mother then back.

Nickolas nodded in concession. "I like to think I favor my father." There was nothing he could do to prevent the disaster they all knew was coming. He prayed it would not involve Jules.

"You have called me to bargain, Lady Brigham." The prince's tone was even, but at the doorway, several onlookers stepped back.

If possible, Lady Brigham's spine went straighter. "You shall marry your pick of my daughters. There are four, all exceptionally lovely and accomplished."

"No," Nickolas gasped.

The prince flicked a hand, and Nickolas's words stuck in his throat, just as the scene had frozen on Lord Filmore's balcony. The prince looked evenly at Lady Brigham. "I cannot. An existing betrothal prevents me."

"An exist—" Lady Brigham's lips pressed closed.

Jules leaned against Nickolas's back as she peered past him, and—with a strange sensation—he understood his voice had returned. He demanded, "Leave off with this fool's game, Mother. It will not end well for anyone involved." Particularly not whichever sister was sent to live with the fae, no matter that it might bring his mother a return to the fortune she so desperately wanted. "I will not allow you to harm them. I will not allow you to continue this ploy." He wasn't certain how he might stop her, as a bargain with a fae prince would supersede any power he held, but he would find a way. Her behavior was beyond reprehensible. He should have stopped her long before so it might never have gone this far.

His mother's cold eyes seemed to dare him to try then shifted to Jules and went ten shades colder. "Her," she told the prince. "Remove that chit from this kingdom to never return. Or turn her to ash. I care not which. As long as she's gone forever."

Before Nickolas could lunge at his mother, he was frozen again by the strange fae magic.

"I cannot," the prince repeated.

Lady Brigham's gaze shot to the prince. "What do you mean you cannot? Do away with the girl. She matters to no one."

The prince gave her a level stare, his words loaded with meaning. "As I've told you, an existing betrothal prevents me."

Nickolas felt himself fall back a step, and he bumped against Jules. *Jules, Jules, Jules*, his heart drummed in a panicked staccato. She made not a sound. The ground felt unsteady beneath Nickolas's feet. He could not seem to reconcile the words he'd heard. They did not seem real.

Outside in the courtyard, there was a rush of murmuring and the muffled beat of marching boots on stone. *The marshal*, the watching crowd murmured. The kingsmen were coming.

The prince's expression remained steady. "You have one final offer to make, Lady Brigham. I suggest you consider it well."

Lady Brigham huffed, the sound reeking of smug victory and delight. "I shall save it," she told him.

Because Lady Brigham had won her boon after all. Jules would no longer interfere, not when she was married to someone else. And if she was married to... when she was taken to... Nickolas could not even make himself think it. It could not be real.

Etta darkened the doorway only an instant before the prince was gone. He must have heard the murmurs as well and known she was coming, but he'd waited, watching the doorway for her appearance. One might not have noticed the small quirk to his brow on an otherwise unchanged face—a clear acknowledgment of the challenge scored in his favor—but Etta had.

She cursed, lunged... and drove her sword into empty air. She stood in the space he had been for one long moment, surrounded by shadows, then seemed to take a steadying breath. When she turned to face the crowd and her men, she was marshal of Westrende once more. "Take them into custody for questioning. All of them."

She gave a hard look to Lady Brigham. "She can wait in the cells."

Nickolas and Jules had been ushered by a pack of the marshal's men into a small room adjacent to Etta's office. They had been left alone, but guards remained posted just outside.

Nickolas sat on the long bench with a sick, defeated sort of feeling in his gut that he did not like at all, while Jules paced in front of him.

She stopped, finally coming to rest before him. When he did not look up, she slid onto the bench, her fine gown smeared with damp earth.

"You were working in the chancery to learn the laws of the kingdom, so that you might find a way to break the betrothal. It had to be here, because you had to understand *our* laws. You never came for asylum. You came to fight." His words were not a question. He did not know how much she might be able to say since her terms had been revealed by the prince. Because the curse, according to Ian, had not been set by Westrende fae. It didn't matter. Nickolas needed to say it.

Jules's reply was so quiet he felt as if he needed to silence his heartbeat to hear. "I had always heard that fae magic did something to a person. That even their speaking could pluck a string so deep inside you that you could feel it vibrate through your bones. That it might eat you up with wanting."

His heartbeat did freeze. He looked at her. She was so close, face bare and hair starting to escape its updo.

She wet her lips. "It did not feel that way to me."

"You were to marry *one of your station*," he said. "A prince."

Jules did not reply. Nickolas shifted to face her, taking her hand in his, their knees touching. She was not for him. "And what of your crime?"

"Murders that I did not commit. They found me standing in—" She swallowed against words she could not seem to speak. "It was the middle of the night. I was in a room that was not my own. Around me, signs of a struggle, blood, scattered feathers."

"Feathers. No bodies?"

She shook her head. "I was accused of bargaining with the fae against the victims, to steal their... so that I might take their... in order to win a privilege which could not be mine unless they were gone."

"Your brothers. The fae curse turned them into birds, and you were blamed."

She nodded. "I asked for the price and was given a... I cannot say. But the price, you now know. I could not do it. But I could not *not* do it."

To break a curse was always an impossible task, Etta had said. Or a choice in which either option was impossible to permit.

"And your people intended to throw you into a cell when you had a curse to break?"

"It was precisely what they intended. So I escaped. Ian helped me. I never would have made it, otherwise. We rode into the night on horses stolen from the king's stable."

"Murders," he said. "How many brothers do you have?"

"Six in all. The others flew free. As long as I'm... if I agree to the terms... they will be well. But Frederick was injured. He could not fly because he had defended me. I bundled him up, kept him at my side the entire journey." She squeezed Nickolas's hand. "I was granted only the standard betrothal period of the fae. That time is running out. If I do not agree, they will be trapped forever inside their new forms. If I do agree, I will be... it will put..." Her face pinched in determination. "Entire kingdoms will be in danger."

"You've been trying to set Frederick free," Nickolas said. "Because you believe you'll not be able to save him before you're whisked away."

"He won't save himself. He refuses to leave me. Seeing him like this, it makes me... I know that I..." Her hand tightened into a fist.

"You're not afraid that you'll be unable to make him whole," Nickolas guessed. "You want him to leave, because you plan to cross the wall and go through with the betrothal."

Her eyes shone in the candlelight. "Not if I can prevent it. It's only that time is running out, and I see no other answer. If I can save my brothers, if they can be returned to themselves..."

His thumb slid over the back of her hand. He could feel

the warmth of her leg where it pressed against his, the touch of her breath over his skin. Unable to stop himself, he reached toward the ring that hung from the chain about her neck, wondering if its magic was what prevented her from speaking freely.

"Nickolas," she said softly. "I must confess something else."

His hand froze.

"My post in the chancery was chosen not simply so that I might have access to research. It allowed me to find those who might be best positioned—or perhaps induced—to help."

His hand lowered to her lap, where his other still cradled hers. He watched her for a long moment. "Why do I have the feeling you're preparing to reveal extortion?"

She did not so much as flinch. "I can help you with your problems. Just as I've promised."

He pulled his hands back. "In exchange for?"

"Not in exchange. You've satisfied our agreement. I can help you, but I need you to help me."

Saints. She *was* extorting him. There was something very wrong with him, because this close, it didn't matter. He wanted to put his lips somewhere on her. Badly. Perhaps the soft bit beneath the corner of her jaw where her pulse jumped. Or an earlobe. Or her mouth. Without a doubt, her mouth. Or, fate save him, that neck.

She's betrothed to the prince of Rivenwilde, he reminded himself. "Still doesn't matter," he mumbled back.

"You're saying you knew my situation," he said. "You mean financially or..." At her level look, he sighed. "What else, then? Did you know I'd be trussed up and—" He sat straighter. "You did know. You knew about the plot against me. That I'd end up in Carvell's courtyard. You—you asked permission to use the man's gardens in front of the *magistrate*."

Her steady gaze never wavered. "There are very few in Westrende who are aware of curses and fae magic. After all, I could not ask Etta or Gideon."

He ran a hand over his face.

She said, "I cannot explain more, but the terms of the bargain are no small thing. I had to use whatever I could to my advantage. I had to find a way out."

Nickolas watched her for a very long moment. Jules was a princess. He should have known. She was too graceful, too clever, too impossibly beautiful to be anything else. He understood what came along with that. Royalty accepted that they must do whatever it took to protect their people. Jules would go to the ends of the earth to see it done. Perhaps she was nearly there already.

Nickolas stood, straightened his torn jacket, and strode to the door. "Gentlemen," he called to the guard outside. "Fetch Lord Beckett, if you please. I have a bargain to uphold."

CHAPTER 15

Jules was in a private room, questioning Lord Beckett about interkingdom law, when Etta and Gideon finally arrived, Frederick's cage in tow.

Nickolas stood. "Did you find the lord from Norcliffe?"

Gideon placed the cage on a table and crossed his arms. "Ian apprehended him. They've both been taken in for questioning."

"He's looking for Jules."

"We gathered," Etta said. "Ian demanded we return the bird to Jules's care and keep her under guard and away from the Norcliffe party until the turn of the moon. What else have you learned?"

"She's betrothed to the prince."

Etta's brows lowered in confusion, but Nickolas did not pause long enough to listen to her remark. "Her brothers were cursed, transformed into birds like Frederick, but there are five more back in her kingdom. No idea where that is yet, as she and Ian won't come clean. She plans to pay the price to break the curse—that is, to marry the prince of Rivenwilde so that her brothers might all live. Apparently, the act will endanger entire kingdoms, but she sees no other way." He tossed up his hands. "And I'm to stay here and cosset her bird."

Etta opened her mouth, closed it, then opened it again. "She means to leave the bird with *you*?"

"Thank you," he said. "For once, a voice of reason. One of you must convince her to change her mind."

Etta straightened. "I can't keep a fae-cursed man-bird. I'm the marshal."

They looked at Gideon.

He said, "I can't do it. I have a dog."

"That doesn't even make sense," Nickolas said. "It should be you most of all. You've proven you can keep an animal alive, for one thing. Two, no one would ever suspect you of breaking the law by harboring an illegal fae-bird-thing." When Gideon only stared at him, Nickolas added, "It should be you. Precisely because you and that bird have identical temperaments."

Gideon narrowed his dark eyes into a glare. Beside him, in the cage, so did Frederick.

"See? There." Nickolas threw up his hands again. "Making my point for me, gentlemen."

The room fell silent for a moment, then Etta asked, "Nickolas, why did you not tell me of your situation?"

He slumped onto the bench with a sigh. "And what? Have you arrest my mother?" He winced. "You *have* arrested her, haven't you?"

"I'm considering it. She did try to sell your sister to the fae. But what about the rest?"

"Adair has information on her. He's been using it to

extort funds and favors from the family since before my father's death."

Gideon's demeanor softened. Or at least, he uncrossed his arms.

Nickolas rubbed an earlobe. "It's true, all of it. We're busted. Flat broke. The coffers are bare. Now that I've admitted it to everyone, our debts will be called in. I'm done for. Probably be tossed from my suite before the end of the week."

Etta stepped closer.

Nickolas's hand dropped to his lap. "The worst thing is, she chose me on purpose. Mess of a thing, Lord Brigham. Perfect sort of target for such a lark." He looked up at Etta. "And I can't even help her." He was a failure once more. A failure when it mattered most. He said, "So, what happens now? You'll cart her back to her kingdom, and we will never see her again? Never know what becomes of her?" Nickolas did not ask if they would hand her over to the fae. Etta might be the one person less capable of that than him.

The door to the room opened, and Jules stepped in. Nickolas stood as her gaze swept the space, a hint of relief showing in her posture when she took in the bird.

"Well," Gideon said, "there is a great deal of paperwork involved in deporting a person. Likely it will take some time to sort out."

Jules's dark eyes slid to his, shining with gratitude.

"Particularly if there's an active investigation," Etta added. She cleared her throat as if even speaking such a betrayal of her duty was painful then turned to face Jules more fully. "Was Lord Beckett any help to you?"

Jules shook her head. "There's no precedent for—no

record of—" She touched the ring resting against her chest. "Nothing of use."

Nickolas glanced at Etta, who gave him an indiscreet nod. Gideon had a book of fae laws. Gideon would help.

"It's been a long day," Jules said. "I'm afraid I've done all I can." She glanced at the wall, but there were no windows to reveal what must have been a very late, very close to full moon. "I'd like to retire."

Gideon nodded. "You'll both come with us. The chancery is the safest place for you right now. We already have a rotation of kingsmen outside your rooms and patrolling the wing."

Jules nodded, but when they arrived at the chancery office after being escorted by the marshal, the chancellor, Ian carrying the bird cage, and about a dozen men, she looked even more dispirited than before.

Etta and Gideon went on to his private office, but Jules stopped before turning to face Nickolas. "My time is nearly up."

Nickolas took her hand in his. "Shall I walk with you?"

Her mouth tightened as if she were holding back emotion. "I think I would like to be alone for a while."

He lifted her hand, bending forward to press a soft kiss on her skin. "Good night, my lady. Know that we will do all we can to help."

Eyes misty, Jules only nodded. It seemed as if she might want to speak, but she did not, only offering him a weak smile before she drew her hand away and turned to go. Nickolas watched as Ian followed with the bird, down the narrow corridor to her room.

"Nickolas?" Etta called from the doorway of Gideon's office.

He cleared his face of concern then turned to join them.

ETTA HAD SECURED the door to Gideon's private office, and the three of them had huddled around his orderly desk. Gideon was as proper and orderly as a man could be, in Nickolas's estimation, but the chancery was stuffed with shelves and stacks and carts. Records of all kinds were housed in every nook and cranny of the ancient wing, and nothing could be done for the dry, dim environment that smelled of aged parchment and spilled ink. The man probably itched to have it all sorted and filed.

He was, after all, twitching like a schoolboy about to get the rod because of the fae relic centered on his desk.

Nickolas let out a low whistle. "I'm no expert, but that looks extraordinarily old and highly illegal."

"It is," Gideon muttered without looking up. "Don't touch it."

Nickolas reclined farther onto the desk, just to annoy him. "Well, someone has to."

Gideon's jaw tightened, but he carefully opened the cover, its binding making a mild crackle of complaint. Nickolas leaned in. The pages had aged well enough and were marked with symbols and lines that seemed to be translated into print. Color dotted the layout sparingly, bits of gold and vibrant red in a few of the illustrations. Not taking his gaze from the writing, Nickolas asked, "Where did you say your father found this?"

Etta shrugged. "I had always assumed he'd taken it off a prisoner. Now, I'm not so certain."

"I've read to here," Gideon said. "The rest will be new."

"And we're looking for..." Nickolas prompted.

"Marriage contracts."

"Right." Something settled in the pit of Nickolas's stomach. It only grew worse as time went on, because Gideon had turned to a section that illustrated fae ceremonies, a full court in attendance beneath a midnight full moon. He did not want to imagine Jules in place of the fae bride, but he could not look away. Trees rose around a clearing, a stone throne centering the edge of the circle like the finest carved marble. Fae creatures of all kinds stood in witness as a prince knelt before his intended.

The office had fallen quiet. Etta placed a gentle hand on Gideon's shoulder. He turned the page.

Pages later, they found what they'd been looking for. Hours after that, Gideon's desk was scattered with documents and scrolls, the three of them poring over contract wording and ancient rites and cross-checking every single aspect of the law.

Gideon sat straighter. "I think we've got it. We only need to verify these last few details."

There was color in Etta's cheeks, and Nickolas could feel a fluttering excitement inside his chest. He didn't want to hope, but there it was, strewn out in front of them—a loophole that might be used to subvert the bargain's terms.

He stood. "We have to tell Jules."

Etta straightened. "There's no use waking her now. We have to prepare, and she's not had enough rest. We'll tell her in the morning."

Gideon stood as well and wrapped the fae book with a

cloth before placing it inside his jacket. When there was a knock at the door, everyone froze.

An instant later, Etta was beside Nickolas, blocking view of the documents on the desk. "Enter," she called.

A soldier stepped in, tall and thin, her dark hair tied into a clean knot above the red-trimmed collar of the uniform of the marshal's office. The soldier gave a practiced salute.

"Report," Etta said.

The soldier glanced at Nickolas and Gideon then hedged, "There's a problem with one of the prisoners."

Etta frowned, hand on her sword hilt. To Gideon and Nickolas, she said, "Best take care of this. I'll meet you both in the morning."

Gideon glanced at the windows, where cockcrow appeared to be less than an hour away.

Etta sighed. "Regardless, I'll return shortly. There's much to do."

At the door, she called over her shoulder, "Get some rest, Nickolas."

Nickolas glanced at Gideon, but Gideon waved him away. "I'll take care of this mess. Do as she says. You'll need it." When Nickolas opened his mouth, Gideon stopped him. "Don't say it."

"You don't even—"

"It doesn't matter. Whatever it is, gratitude or mockery, I don't need it right now. Jules needs saved. That's all I've room for."

At that, Nickolas found his words had slunk away. He only nodded, turning to leave the room as Gideon resumed his work. At the door, though, Nickolas looked back, his fingers wrapping around the heavy oak slab. "Gideon?"

Gideon glanced up, chancellor through and through.

"Did you know she was a princess?"

His tone was subdued. "I only knew she needed help."

Nickolas rapped his knuckles once on the wood then inclined his head and pulled the door shut behind him.

The chancery's main chamber was dark and silent. Dawn would soon light the high windows, but until then, it was very large, very quiet, and despite the many kingsmen posted outside the chancery entrance, Nickolas felt very alone.

He should be sleeping. Etta was right. But he couldn't stop thinking about what she'd said about Jules needing rest. Jules had not seemed especially sleepy when she'd left them, not considering the way he'd seen her nap just about anywhere once she had the notion. She had only seemed subdued. It was the manner, he thought suddenly, of a person saying farewell.

His feet moved toward her corridor of their own accord. The knot in his stomach had hollowed out. She was gone. He was sure of it. She'd done something foolish—something brave and foolish and horrible—and slipped away in the night to the forest.

Jules was going to cross the boundary into fae.

When he was half the distance to her corridor, Nickolas's eye caught a flicker of movement outside. He stopped to squint at the window across the space and made out a lantern light moving through the courtyard. Two men were tugging along something he couldn't quite make out. It was small and dark and... about the size of a woman.

Jules hadn't left. She'd been *taken*.

The thought had no more than registered when a call came from one of the guards in the corridor near the chancery entrance. Nickolas did not wait to hear what followed. He was already running, dodging past a scroll cart and leaping over the long table that separated him and the courtyard. Canisters and jars clattered behind him as they rolled to the floor, then the cool night air hit his skin, and he was gone at a full run.

CHAPTER 16

The courtyard was dark, shifting with shadows. Nickolas ran straight for the men, light on his feet as he drew his sword. One of the men had a familiar stride, the other too bulky to be likely to fight with any grace. He would take the smaller one first with a leg strike then pray the other let go of Jules to face him. She didn't look right, her movements off. He wasn't certain how they'd gotten past her guard, but if she was hurt, if they'd done anything to harm her, Nickolas would not need the kingsmen at his back. He would bring the men to justice himself.

He shot past a topiary, and his step nearly faltered at a niggling thought about where the kingsmen were—because surely there had been three dozen about the chancery— but the familiar figure lifted the lantern and looked back, letting Nickolas see his face.

William Adair.

A nasty word came from Nickolas's lips as he closed the distance, but William kept moving. The men were nearly to the gate on the far side of the courtyard. Nickolas would catch them before they made it. He was only strides away. But when the men reached the shadows cast by a massive arbor, they stopped and turned.

Something was wrong. Very, very wrong. Nickolas fell to a stop, too late and too close. Facing him, opposite William, stood one of Lady Brigham's men. The figure between them could not seem to keep its form.

Dawn light crept over the courtyard, coloring the leaves bronze and tipping the statuary with gold and pink. Surrounded by fruit trees and daffodils, slightly behind the men, stood the figure of a petite woman, her visage flickering between glamour and fae. She was not Jules.

Nickolas was already backing up when the first set of hands grabbed him from behind. He spun, tearing his mangled jacket and striking swords with a fourth man. Nickolas had trained kingsmen, so he knew how to use a weapon. One swing gave him distance, and the second struck an assailant in the thigh. He was moving, eyes on his surroundings, but there was no way out other than to fight.

The men had never been after Jules. They'd come for Nickolas. And he was penned in, led into a trap baited by glamour. His mother's men were working with William, all in league with the Rivenwilde woman.

He had no time to think. A sweep, slash, and dodge, and two men were down. The largest came at him from behind while another tried to pin him between the fae and the trees at sword-point while William watched from a distance, but Nickolas was too fast.

The big man came at him again, and with a crush, the brute was knocked to his knees. One of the wounded rose, without his weapon, and Nickolas caught a blow to the cheek before he was once again down to two opponents. The large man grunted when he was cracked by the hilt of Nickolas's sword and stumbled back for a moment that left Nickolas free to make quick work of the other. A few more clumsy attempts by the final brute, and he was down as well, leaving his mark on Nickolas by way of a few busted knuckles.

Nickolas's knuckles stung and burned as he turned to William, his face hard as his grip tightened on his sword.

Before he'd made a step toward the man, William held up a hand. "Lest you attempt anything dangerous, I should warn you that the lady here has been granted leave to go after Jules, should I not be able to pay her."

Three of the men were rising to their feet, weapons shifting in preparation. The one with longer hair held a rope and a large piece of canvas. Apparently, they meant to haul him away. It truly was a trap. Capture, not kill. He would be used... *For what?* A ransom plot, perhaps. And if he forced William's hand, Jules might be used in the same way. If they'd discovered she was a princess...

"You'll never touch her," Nickolas said.

"And yet, I see that you have ceased your advance." William clicked his tongue. "You should have noticed by now that we've the run of the courtyard. Fae glamour can be a marvelous aid when it's on your side. Why, with this disguise, she'd be in and out before a single soul noticed. She's already managed to evade the entire guard." William gave him his most level tone. "Touch me, and she gets the girl. It's part of our bargain. She wins either way."

The fae woman grinned. Her true form was dark and willowy, long hair loose in disordered strands. She wore the gown of a lady, but Nickolas had no reference to be certain of her status among the fae. He'd only ever seen a prince.

William took in how Nickolas's grip shifted on the sword hilt and said, "Yes. There you go. Now, gentlemen."

Around him, the men drew closer. Nickolas lifted his weapon, but it was clear there was no way out. He could not let Jules be harmed, and even if he killed every man in the courtyard, he could not touch the Adair heir. He never should have left the safety of the chancery. He'd been a fool to step foot where he was not protected. All he was left with was the chance to see the fae woman removed from the castle grounds. The sky was lightening. His racing heart was wearing down.

The big man moved for him.

"Wait!" Nickolas called. The man did wait, and Nickolas took a careful step backward. He held up a hand. "Just, hold a moment." He could not do it. He could not allow himself to be taken into William's custody. But there was no way out. There was no way to gain a true victory.

But he couldn't stomach the idea of being hauled off by henchmen again. And *by the wall*, what if William spread the tale? Even if his mother found a way to raise the ransom, Nickolas would never be able to show his face at court. His pride would not stand for it.

"All right," he said.

The men looked confused.

"I'll go willingly." He raised a finger to point directly at each of the men. "But I want it known that this is *not* a kidnapping."

They glanced at each other.

Nickolas pointed at the man with the ropes and cloth. "To be clear, I will be voluntarily climbing into that sack."

IN SHORT ORDER, Nickolas had been placed on the rough cloth, his hands and feet tied "just to be safe." Three of the men stood in a straggle around him and William. The fae woman lingered in the shadows. As per Nickolas and William's agreement, she would be paid her due once they arrived outside of the castle.

The fourth man sat nearby, his face pale and palms pressed to a gaping wound on his thigh, breeches soaked with blood.

"Leave him," William said. "He's useless to us now."

"But the kingsmen will find him," the brute argued.

William gave the man a quelling look. "Then he should not have gotten *stabbed*, should he? Next time, he will know better."

The brute parroted the look and the tone. "Then they'll tie the crime to me as his associate, won't they?"

William's jaw clenched. "Have it your way." He pointed at the scraggliest. "You, stay with him. Find a way to get him out of this courtyard before"—he glanced at the sky—"well, I'd say you've about five minutes."

With a grand gesture to the brute, William said, "Now, if you wouldn't mind getting on with it before we're all tied to the crime."

"Getting on with it" evidently entailed wrapping the cloth tightly around Nickolas and throwing a sack over his head. Glamour gone, they had to remove him from the premises without being seen. He was tossed quite unceremoniously over the big man's shoulder.

Bound as he was, he could make out only an estimation of their route. They'd gone through a courtyard gate, over the stone walkways that surrounded the wing, then snaked through a castle corridor that Nickolas guessed must have been lesser used.

Once they were outside, the fae woman paid and gone, Nickolas was thrown over a pack horse. They rode at a solid clip, not nearly as far as Nickolas had expected. When he was pulled down from the horse, he had a sick, sinking sensation in his gut. There was the *snap* and *crunch* of underbrush beneath the men's boots, thick enough that it could not be a courtyard or garden, close enough a ride that it must be the forest that bordered the kingdom.

When they'd traveled some distance, Nickolas was set on his feet onto soft earth. His hands were left bound, but they'd given him his legs to lead him by his elbows through the trees. The way was rough, and a nearby chuckle escaped Adair whenever Nickolas stumbled. The smaller of the two henchmen muttered about their surroundings, and Nickolas thought he made out the words *sinister* and *unnatural*. Eventually, they stopped, and Nickolas was pushed onto the greensward on his rear. A murmur of *Rivenwilde prince* came from the smaller man, and the ground seemed to rumble beneath Nickolas. It sounded as if the men took a wary step back.

The sack was pulled from Nickolas's head. He blinked against the dust and the early morning light, his hair falling about his face. William stood before him, dapper in his finery as if they'd not just traipsed through the woods and evidently unaware of the fae creatures that crawled about his feet.

Nickolas, however, could not seem to take his eyes from them.

Catlike and spiky, the things rolled and hissed, one circling near William's boot with its eyes on the man's watch fob. Nickolas had not been so close to one before. He tried to scoot away but could not, given the cloth tangled around him and the rope tying his hands and feet. He glanced up at William, who seemed confused by the look on his face.

"Are you well, Nicky? It was just a little ride in a sack. You've done much worse on a lark." He swatted at something near his ear. "Was it the fae woman? I know, truly, that was unfair. Very unsporting of me. But I must always hedge my bets. You know that."

"Fae," Nickolas wheezed. William was taking him to the fae. No ransom would be enough. Nickolas's return would require a bargain. His gaze darted to the trees, where glowing eyes stared back at him—much larger, much more dangerous creatures waiting their turn. He was grateful that it was daylight, at least. "You bargained with fae. Just to get back at me?"

William had not yet laid eyes on the prince. Nickolas was sure of it. There was no other way the man would be able to stand so calmly among the creatures. The henchmen had not either. His mother must have only heard Jules's words before the prince had used his magic to still the room. If any of them could see what Nickolas was seeing, they would run.

William lowered into a squat, bringing him close to Nickolas. "Oh," he said. "I'm not doing this to punish you.

I'm quite glad you're out of contention. It will make things easier for me. Everyone says Princess Mireille has set her cap at you. Can't hurt not to have you around." His voice lowered, tinged with self-satisfaction. "But this... I'm doing this for your mother. She's promised me a great deal in exchange for the task."

Had Nickolas thought he was beyond surprise, the rogue in a gentleman's jacket had proved him wrong again. Lady Brigham was conspiring with their extortionist. He did not know what she meant to gain, but he realized he should not have been surprised. His mother had tried to trade one of his sisters to the fae only the day before, after all. It did not sting any less. "You know you cannot trust her."

William smiled. "That is the beauty of this deal, my friend. I do not *need* to trust her. Your dear mother has found herself locked, however temporarily, inside a cell." He pointed at himself then the other two men. "We make the trade, return to Westrende, and should your mother not uphold her end of the agreement, all the spoils go to me."

One of the other men grunted, and William added, "And them. Of course, the spoils will also go to them." The wink he gave Nickolas made clear the men would never see a single coin.

William leaned down and shoved the sack roughly over Nickolas's head again. "Take care, old chap."

AFTER NICKOLAS'S captor called the prince's name, low words were spoken between William and the prince, barely skirting the bounds of civility. It was not long before William and the henchmen were dismissed. There was a moment of stillness in which Nickolas thought he heard a sigh, then the prince spoke low words of his own, and a new voice followed.

"Take him," the prince said.

A single hand took hold of Nickolas's arm and led him in the direction that he knew was the wall. His feet dug in automatically, but the hand somehow held more strength than it ought. It drew him forward, unyieldingly, and Nickolas sensed the moment they stepped over the Rive.

When Nickolas was a boy, he'd once leapt into a pond on a dare. It had been the dead of winter, and the moment his skin touched the icy water, shock stole through his entire being. He'd barely made it back to the shore that day, shivering and stiff and uttering nonsense.

That shock was nothing to crossing the boundary. For one instant, it felt as if his body were submerged, overwhelmed with pressure and sensation and the intense desire to reach the surface. Then they were through and the sensation gone. He did feel the urge to utter a few nonsensical noises, but otherwise, it was as if the sensation had never happened at all.

The hand on his arm urged him forward, and the path beneath his feet suddenly had the feel of polished marble. He had the sense he'd been moved by fae magic, as the prince had done when he'd taken Nickolas and Jules from the Filmore balcony. A short flight of stairs followed before Nickolas felt warmth and the still air of indoors. He thought he detected the scent of flowers when the hand leading him stopped, giving a gentle squeeze that Nickolas took as an indicator to stay put.

So there Nickolas stood.

"Get that off." The voice belonged to the prince and was tinged with annoyance.

The cloth covering Nickolas's head was removed, his wrists unbound. He stood in the center of a massive entrance hall, its fine, smooth stone reminiscent of the glamour that obscured the filigree wall, every corner and trim piece impossibly intricate. Opulent and grand, it rose three stories, with carved marble stairs and great open archways overlooking the floor. Thin vines trailed over surfaces like living sculpture, flowering magenta and violet beneath the open ceiling so far above.

Nickolas blinked hard several times in an attempt to make what he was seeing disappear. It did not. He was inside a fae palace. The prince stood before him, evidently waiting for Nickolas to grant his attention. Nickolas held up a single finger while continuing to gape.

He could not quite believe it. His own mother had traded him to the fae. He'd been delivered to the prince himself. He was standing inside a *Rivenwilde* palace.

"Lord Brigham," the prince said dourly. "I do have other matters to attend this afternoon."

Nickolas blinked at the man, realizing his finger was still in the air and that his hands were a bit numb from their bindings. He dropped the finger and rubbed his hands together surreptitiously.

The corner of the prince's eye twitched irritably. "Noal will show you to your rooms and provide a fresh wardrobe. He will be available should you require aught else."

Nickolas glanced from the tall, smartly dressed man who had untied his hands to the prince. "My rooms?"

The twitch appeared again, possibly more intensely. "As I said."

His gaze darting across the space once more, Nickolas said, "I'm not... you'll not put me in a cell?"

A flat expression crossed the prince's face, as if put off by the idea, but he said only, "There is no need to bind you. Should you leave this palace, you will no longer be under my protection. That, I believe you will find, is incentive enough."

Nickolas shot a glance at the other fae, Noal, whose expression was a bit more telling. What it told Nickolas was that he did not want to discover what awaited him in the fae wilds.

The prince waited until his attention returned then said, "I suggest you take dinner in your rooms. You may not find the entire court as welcoming as its prince." He inclined his head before turning to go then disappeared through a massive arched doorway into another room.

It had not been disagreeable advice. Noal led Nickolas —free of bonds and free of mask—through the palace to a suite of rooms. The man was as precise as any of Westrende's top staff and had deftly introduced Nickolas to the suite as his bath and wardrobe were prepared by a few bustling fae.

Nickolas and Noal stood alone in the windowless sitting room. Nickolas ran a hand over his face. A window or balcony would do him no good in any case, not when he could not traverse the wilds on his own. "What happens now?"

"That is for the prince to decide," Noal said.

Nickolas considered the words for a long moment, uncertain of the etiquette for any part of his situation, then asked, "How much did she get for me?"

Noal frowned. "In the end, it is often as much as they deserve."

Sick at the thought, Nickolas only nodded. It did not matter how much his mother received in her bargain, only what dealing with the fae would cost her. And that, he was afraid, was more than she would be willing to pay. "And what's he to do with me, this prince?"

"Feed, clothe, and provide shelter, as per the laws of hospitality."

Nickolas narrowed his gaze. "Any chance I could get a copy of those laws?"

"It would be unnecessary, given that you are bound only by the laws of your kingdom. We, however, are bound by the laws of hospitality, as we are with all laws of Riven-wilde, and by the curse."

"The curse?"

"I cannot answer that. As I suspect you already know that those bound by a curse may not lay out the details of its terms, it should not come as a surprise." Noal's thumb slid over a knuckle, where his gloved hands were held precisely before his waist. "It is not so unlike the terms of the laws of hospitality."

"How so?"

One of Noal's gloved fingers twitched. "Your protection under the laws of hospitality protects the prince as well. You'll not be able to speak a word of what you've seen here."

Nickolas's breath caught in his chest.

The fae inclined his head. "Lord Brigham, if that is all."

"You have my gratitude," Nickolas managed. He bowed slightly, though he wasn't certain how much of a lord he even was in the current situation.

Once Noal and the others had gone, inconceivably leaving the door to his suite unlocked, Nickolas cleaned off the mud and the muck gathered during his journey through the forest and before, when he had rolled around the courtyard building with Ian. It seemed impossible that, having had no chance to change or sleep, he was still wearing his clothes from the ball—the lovely and perfect and entirely ill-conceived ball. Nickolas sat on the edge of a chaise, staring at the finely woven rug beneath his feet. He had not allowed himself to recall the night before, had not dwelt on his last moments with Jules. Her grief and fear when she'd been discovered by the Norcliffe lord, her resignation when she'd left him standing in the chancery.

William and his mother would meet a much worse fate than Nickolas for what they'd done, but he could not fathom the distress his disappearance would cause Etta and the others. He could not guess what they would be asked to sacrifice to see his return. The price would be exorbitant.

He could not expect them to pay it.

The thoughts swirled through his head and tore at his heart, and it was there, on the fae chaise with his head in his hands, that Nickolas succumbed to sleep.

When he woke, it was with the sensation of having lost direction. The remaining candles burned low, and the unfamiliar room took on the eerie glow of half-light. He was still in shirtsleeves, the fae wardrobe laid over an adjacent chair. On a nearby table waited a plate of food along with a decanter. The pitcher and basin had been refreshed, and freshly polished boots rested near the clothes.

Nickolas stood, stumbled over the ragged jacket he'd dropped to the floor, and made his way to the door of the suite. It remained unlocked. He opened it and glanced down the empty corridor before stepping out of his room. At the far end was a set of wide double doors carved with ancient script. As if drawn to it, Nickolas moved through the corridor, careful of every doorway he passed, even though each was closed.

When he stood before the doorway, he could not quite bring his lifted hand to touch the carvings. While much of the palace and its furnishings felt clean and modern, the doors seemed as ancient as the script. Finely shaped vines trailed over the words, a phrase he thought translated to something like *balance must be kept*, though one of the words might instead have been *justice*. Brow furrowed, he studied the design in grain that appeared to be hawthorn, darkened with age. A bit of moss covered one of the symbols, and he reached up to brush it away.

The doors fell open beneath his touch.

Nickolas glanced behind him, but the corridor remained empty. Before him was a room that seemed untouched by time. It was a massive open space, lit dimly by narrow gaps in a style of drapery that had not been fashionable for centuries. On high walls, the paintings and frames were of a similar sort, and centering the room was a hawthorn pedestal carved in a manner that appeared to be rooted to the floor, live vines and flowers reaching up to wrap around the base.

Upon the pedestal sat an hourglass, its sands nearly drained. That same sensation of being drawn forward had

Nickolas moving, but one foot forward gave him the sense that the threshold was a boundary—similar to the wall over the Rive, which he had not liked at all.

He stepped backward, leaving the room to its peace. When the doors fell closed once more, Nickolas took two steps farther away. He turned, wiping his damp palm on his trouser leg, and surveyed the space.

At the other end of the corridor was a large open archway, soft with evening light. He traversed the distance just as carefully, passing the still-open door to his own room. He heard no sounds or indications of other occupants, even from the rooms below.

The air was cool through the open archway, its marble smooth where he placed his palm to the frame. He leaned forward, staring into a courtyard three stories below. There were no platforms or trellises, not even a statue or pool. Only the stone and the earth and a fall certain to break a good deal of bone.

His gaze lifted to the opposite wall of the courtyard and beyond, where as far as he could see, sprawling estate houses peeked from a landscape more green and lush than anything Nickolas had ever known. But in the distance, at the edge of the forest, stood a pyre as tall as the trees. Smaller pyres stood scattered around it, and countless indistinct shapes moved through the clearing in a manner that was not unlike the staff at Westrende when preparing for an event.

Dread sank into him as his eyes rose to the sky.

"Moontide," said a voice at his ear.

Nickolas jumped, nearly tumbling through the window before he managed to turn his back against the frame. He had been alone in the corridor, he was sure of it, and yet the fae woman was only inches from him, pressing close enough he could still feel the breath as her words had brushed his skin.

She was unusually tall, her features sharp, the corners of her wide lips and dark eyes tipped upward in a smile. She wore a silk gown and jewels in her hair, but strapped at her side was a double-edged dagger that appeared well-used. When she showed her teeth, he had to still the sudden urge to run.

"Are you lost, little lord?"

Nickolas was not proud of how long it took him to get out "I am a guest of the prince."

She leaned nearer, voice dropping to a whisper. "As am I."

He tried to slide casually along the wall, away from the open archway.

She sauntered in the same direction. Her eyes twinkled like an actual, literal spark of light. Nickolas froze, his elbow brushing where the wall met a corner.

She said, "I can take you closer, little lord. Take you to see the festivities below. Would you like that?"

"I'm afraid I must decline."

"Must you?" Her gaze flicked over his disheveled attire. "You do not look bound to me. Come now. It's not far. Only just outside."

Outside the palace, where he had no protection from the laws of hospitality. Where the prince and Noal had assured him he did not want to go. *Noal.* That was what he should do—call for help. Noal would come, surely, just as others had called on the prince. But Nickolas did not know if calling a fae would indebt him in some way. "I must prepare for dinner. If you'll allow me to make my farewell—"

Before he could even attempt a bow, the fae moved closer. "Give me your name, little lord, so that I might speak it."

"I—"

"My lord," said a voice from down the corridor.

Nickolas and the woman looked up to find Noal standing before the entrance to Nickolas's rooms. Nickolas was unsettled to realize the woman's fingers had curled into a grip on the chest of his shirt, and he'd not even noticed.

Noal said, "It is time to make ready for the evening's event."

Nickolas sagged a little in relief then hurried to slide past the woman and toward Noal, the woman's grip dragging free of him. When he reached the doorway, he glanced back to give a perfunctory dip of the head in case there was some rule of propriety he was unaware he might be breaking, but she was watching him with a long-nailed finger flicking irritably at the tip of her knife.

Inside, Noal tutted at the state of Nickolas's wardrobe.

"Would she have harmed me?" Nickolas asked.

Noal gestured to urge him toward the basin and fresh attire. "You will find not everyone at court is as welcoming as the prince."

"He said that already."

Noal handed Nickolas a fresh shirt. "The prince is not known to lie."

CHAPTER 17

Nickolas was dressed in a fine suit, well-fitting boots, and a too-tight cravat. He had retied the cravat several times, but the sensation of being strangled would not seem to cease. When Noal had deemed him "well enough," they made their way to a private study that was quiet, dimly lit, and painfully impressive. It gave Nickolas a little pang of envy, and he thought he might have preferred the strangled feeling.

Before Noal made their introduction, the prince laid down his quill and looked up at them. He seemed to draw a resigned breath then stood, pulled on his jacket, and slipped the folded parchment into a pocket of his vest. "Lord Brigham."

Nickolas bowed.

The prince came out from behind the large desk then crossed the room and faced him. "It is moontide. The lady Jules and I are to be wed."

There was a long moment of silence, wherein Nickolas

was unsure if he'd spoken a word in reply. In his head, many, many words had been spoken. Shouted, even. Words like *no* and *the deuce you will*. But then *moontide* sank in, and Nickolas could only see the illustrations they'd found in Etta's fae book, Gideon's fingers tracing the figure of a bride and groom beneath the light of a full moon. Their potential loophole must not have worked out. She would have to make her impossible choice. *It has nothing to do with you*, he told himself. Because to Jules, Nickolas would be no one. Between his mother's actions, the family debt, and a fae bargain, Nickolas might not even be a lord. He did not understand why the prince was telling him, but Nickolas understood well enough where he stood.

Jules was a princess. She might be marrying a fae, but he was a prince—one equal to her station. Nickolas's entire chest went tight. He could not think of her standing where he was, trapped in Rivenwilde and beholden to fae whims. He didn't know whether she might be locked in a room or paraded about at court events, but it didn't matter. It was all untenable.

The prince said, "She has agreed to the terms on the condition that the ceremony is held in the heart of the forest, near the Rive." His dark gaze slid momentarily away, toward a wall of richly bound books. "And that once the ceremony has concluded, you will be set free."

The weight in Nickolas's stomach felt as if it might drag him to the ground. He was being pulled apart, bit by bit. Jules's terms had already been named, which meant she had sacrificed something new. Something besides the breaking of a curse.

"What did you take from her in return?"

The prince gazed toward the ceiling as he requested, "Noal."

Noal retrieved a draped object from a side table then held it where Nickolas could see. The drape was pulled away to reveal a finely woven enclosure holding a familiar dull-gray bird.

"Frederick," Nickolas breathed.

"Yes." It did not sound as if the prince took any joy in the trade.

Nickolas asked, "Why?"

The prince's gaze came back to Nickolas. "She has no more choice in the matter than I."

"So you set me free but trap her brother..."

"He will only be as trapped as a princess of Rivenwilde."

Nickolas swallowed his response, struck by the bird's wide, dark eyes. Jules would not be alone. She would have a companion. She would hate it, but Frederick had chosen to stay with her time and again. He would likely choose the same outcome himself. It begged the question of why the prince had named it as his price.

"There will be a ceremony, and you are required to attend," the prince explained. "I do not wish to bind you as your people have. Will you give your word to remain under my command?"

Nickolas watched him for a long moment. The prince looked tired and not from lack of sleep. Whatever else he was, whatever deals he'd made with Jules, he was still fae. Nickolas said, "With respect, even I am not fool enough to go willingly into such a bargain."

"Very well." The prince gave his gaze to Noal, and then with the dizzying sensation of falling from an unsafe height, the lot of them were swept away, no longer in the dim study but standing out of doors, near the ancient filigree wall that rose from the Rive.

It was past nightfall, but the clearing was lit with torches and scattered with flowering vines that had not been there before. At the center of the clearing was an altar, standing before a trellis draped with night-blooming flowers. A dozen armed fae men and women waited with their backs to the wall, naked hands at their sides and eyes on the forest. Flickering shadows danced among the trees, where Nickolas could see with his newly gifted sight, and the forms of shadowy creatures appeared to dance as well.

It did not seem the dance of a celebration, he thought, as much as it was like the preparations the king's guard made before contests of skill. But Nickolas was within the Westrende borders, through the wall once more, and his skin felt alight with the desire to act. To run, to fight, to make any attempt at defeating what fate had in store.

Nickolas's hands had no more than tightened into fists before the prince made a gesture that prevented any attempt at all. Roots burst from the ground around him. He leapt back, but the magic surrounded him, shooting upward to weave dark, woody strands into form. When the form was complete, the magic abruptly fell still. A few small clods of dirt fell to the earth with a dull, muffled *thump*.

Nickolas's gaze met the prince's through the tracery. He'd been placed inside a cage, a massive, man-sized enclosure not unlike the ones in Lady Narine's aviary. "What fresh abyss is this?" he whispered.

Beside him, Noal hooked Frederick's cage to a root near Nickolas's head. The bird grunted a similar complaint.

Noal stepped back to stand beside the prince, whose distaste was evident. "I would have much preferred a spoken vow."

Noal's reply was sanguine. "It will encourage them to save him. They'll be far less likely to attempt any deception this way."

The prince's face pinched. "Human trickery does grow tiresome."

Noal hummed in agreement.

"Truly," Nickolas challenged, but his protests went unheard as a call echoed from within the trees. It sounded predatory. Every fae in the clearing looked toward the forest. From the nearby brush, something catlike moved. Nickolas reached through a space in the roots, opened the door to Frederick's cage, and drew the bird to his chest. For once, Frederick was quiet.

What came through the trees was no beast at all but a petite figure wearing a simple muslin dress. Frederick made a croak of protest, and Nickolas realized he'd squeezed the bird too tightly to his chest. Relaxing his grip, he watched with Frederick as Jules came further into view.

She might have been dressed simply, but she held the bearing of a princess, through and through. Shoulders back, head high, she strode with casual purpose toward the prince. She looked impossibly beautiful, features lit by the moon like the first night Nickolas had met her. Behind her walked Ian, his pace steady. He wore a sword at his hip and carried a small valise.

Nickolas did not think Jules had seen him, but when she approached the prince, she disregarded his elegant bow and said, "Release him."

The prince looked up at her mid-bow, glanced at Nickolas, then straightened. "My lady, it is—"

"Release. Him."

The prince cleared his throat.

Jules did not flinch. "It is not as if you should be concerned for his escape. Not when you might move from here to there and snatch him back in an instant. What could you possibly be afraid of? You're the prince of the Riven Court."

The prince's mouth went into a hard line. He flicked a hand, and the roots snapped around Nickolas, falling to the ground in broken bits. His tone was level. "Is that all, or do you wish to lay additional demands upon a prince of the Riven Court?"

She appeared to swallow. She still did not look toward Nickolas or Frederick. "For now, that is all."

The prince's jaw flexed. He turned, proffering his arm so that she might be led to the trellis. Nickolas knew this, because the cursed illustration from Etta's fae book had been reminding him of the scene every few seconds. Frederick made a miserable little sound, but Nickolas could not seem to make a sound at all. Magic prevented him from saying aloud that as the cage around him had broken, thin fingers of vine rose behind the cover of grass to wrap themselves tightly over and around the ankles of Nickolas's borrowed boots.

The prince had not lied. It did not mean he was worthy of trust.

The prince led Jules beneath a radiant moon to stand framed by the trellis. Ian moved toward Nickolas as if merely finding an inconspicuous spot from which to watch. He sat the valise on the ground at his side, without glancing at Nickolas even once. A thin gold chain glinted at the bag's clasp. Two of the fae standing near the wall had never taken their eyes off of Ian, and three more had a solid watch on Nickolas.

The prince withdrew the folded parchment from his vest and laid it on the altar. He picked up the quill and handed it first to Jules. She took it carefully, glancing first at the prince then at the wall. The quill shifted in her hand. She lifted the parchment to read.

"It is accurate," the prince said quietly. "To the letter."

"I'll just... I need to read it first."

The prince gestured that she should proceed but gave a significant glance at the moon. Time was running out.

Jules adjusted the parchment. Shifted the quill. Glanced once more at the wall.

Frederick began to cough.

Jules's gaze shot to the bird. It was nearly time. The moon was high, and Frederick's curse would soon be enduring. The only way to save him was to sign the contract and marry the prince.

"Here," Ian said. "Let me take him." He stepped closer, kicking the valise over as he took Frederick from Nickolas's determined grip.

Jules's gaze brushed Nickolas for one heartbeat, then it was gone. Head down, she pressed quill to paper.

Nickolas went hot. He knelt automatically, unwilling to let a single soul see his face, and made a production of righting the valise. His fingers caught on the chain of the necklace, and a strange sensation rolled through him. He froze, in fear that one of the fae guards might have seen. Then he wrapped his finger twice around the delicate chain and pulled before slipping the ring that hung from it into his palm. Face still hot, he rose to stand, not daring to move his feet.

Because his boots, his voice, and the magic's hold on him was free. The fisted hand at his side held Jules's magic ring.

CHAPTER 18

Eyes on Jules and the prince, Nickolas was gripped by both the intense desire to stop the ceremony and to let it go ahead. Stop it because it was madness to let her marry a fae prince. Let it go ahead because, beside him, Ian held Jules's brother, who would be stuck in the form of a bird forever.

It was just as Etta had said. Neither choice was tenable. They had failed to find a way to break the curse.

A wind picked up in the clearing, whispering through the leaves as if warning of time running out. If Nickolas chose incorrectly, he might condemn Jules and her brother to a lifetime of misery, but it was clear Jules was delaying. Ian had made certain Nickolas had possession of the ring for a reason, and his mistress's hand could not quite seem to make the final stroke on her contract.

Nickolas drew a breath, crushed the ring in his palm, then pulled the sword from the scabbard at Ian's hip in one swift movement. The prince did not even turn around, only flicked his hand in a gesture Nickolas was sure the move was meant to still him. It did not. He was half the distance to the altar when six of the fae guards came off their positions near the wall. He was two strides farther by the time they reached him, and when the prince finally did turn, Jules dipped in a move not unlike a curtsy then rose again with a dagger she'd evidently pulled from beneath her skirts—pressed firmly to the prince's side. Well placed, in fact, to drive upward beneath his ribs.

A sword clashed against Nickolas's—the fae guard not as easily managed as Jules's coachman or his mother's henchmen—and Nickolas was pushed a step backward. He swung again, pivoted, and was nearly struck with a blow that might have severed his arm.

"Stop them," Jules commanded the prince just as Nickolas swung again.

The prince's gaze rolled skyward. Nickolas had the sense that he was not checking the state of the moon.

The prince called, "Halt," and the fae guard drew back but kept Nickolas surrounded. The prince glanced over his shoulder then corrected his gaze lower, at Jules. He said, "No harm may come to the prince of the Riven Court."

Jules stared at him in earnest. "Oh, that warning applies only to citizens of Westrende. As you're aware, I am not a citizen of Westrende."

The prince's eyes pressed closed. The expression put Nickolas in mind of their nanny after she'd been locked with his sisters inside a single room for three days straight. The prince's tone was not a great deal different from the nanny's either when he said, "As you may also be aware, there remains just over a quarter hour before your curse sets its course. If you intend to stab a fae prince, I suggest you choose one you are not meant to marry."

She said, "Let him go. When he and Ian are out of sight, then I will sign, and this will all be over."

"Spoken like the most eager of brides," the prince muttered. He gestured toward Nickolas. "You are as free to leave as you've been this entire time, Lord Brigham."

Nickolas opened his mouth to explain that he had, in fact, not been free at all, when a new voice came from the edge of the clearing.

"Not so fast."

The prince turned away from Jules, who doggedly followed with her well-aimed blade, and glared in the direction of the trees. "Lady Ostwind," he said. "I would like to remind you that this entire affair is none of your concern."

Etta tromped closer, sword in hand, Gideon at her back with an armload of documents and, nonsensically, Princess Mireille with three of her courtiers behind them.

Etta pointed at the filigree wall. "That's where you're wrong, because everything on this side of the Rive is my concern."

The prince's mouth turned down. "We are only on this side of the wall because your..." He cleared his throat. "Because the lady Jules has required it. Had I my preference, we would be nowhere near Westrende."

Etta drew to a stop less than ten paces from the prince, the others fanning out beside her. "Jules is no mere lady, and you know it."

The prince's jaw flexed. "That is her secret to keep. It was never mine to bandy about. And it is her decision whether to proceed with..." His words fell off once more, then he glanced at Jules. "Have you changed your mind about the ceremony or only the terms of Lord Brigham's release?"

Jules adjusted her grip on the dagger. "It is no secret that I do not wish to marry you. But I have no choice in the matter."

"Actually." Gideon stepped forward, every eye in the clearing suddenly on him. He cleared his throat then withdrew the fae book from his jacket.

The prince made a pained sound, but Nickolas found himself stepping closer. The fae surrounding him did not move.

Gideon spoke only to Jules. "The price named was to marry one of your station. It was not specific to the prince of the Riven Court."

The prince said, "While this is all very dramatic, I will remind you that her time is running out." The *there are no other princes present* was heavily implied.

Princess Mireille sidled up to Gideon and gave a little wave to Jules. Jules's color had gone off, but Mireille did not seem to pay it mind. She said, "I heard about what happened at the ball and insisted I be allowed to help. Jules is from a neighboring kingdom to my own, and I told Gideon the stories we had heard regarding her father."

"Namely," Gideon explained, "that the king had fallen under the sway of a fae queen. The very one, I suspect, who cursed each of the king's heirs and left only Jules to escape."

"Frederick was the bravest brother." Princess Mireille's gaze searched the clearing until she found Ian holding the bird. "Oh, is that him? He's darling." Frederick made a chiding hiss, but Mireille's attention had already returned to the prince. "Ian told us that while Frederick managed to save Jules from a similar fate, he was injured. The brothers were presumed dead, and the court blamed Jules, but many among the staff refused to believe it."

The prince said flatly, "Then the palace became plagued by large white birds, five to be precise, determined to ruin every event held at the fae queen's behest."

The princess's grin widened. "Exactly that. Talk began that they were the spirits of the brothers, come to seek revenge. But the sixth brother, it was said, had somehow escaped the queen's curse. Tales began that he would return one day to vanquish the fae queen. As you can imagine, she took no joy in that."

"I need not imagine," the prince replied.

Mireille's right eye pinched in something vaguely wink-like before her gaze flicked back to Jules. "Gideon told me Frederick was well, and I'm so pleased. But I knew there was more to the story. In fact, Lord Holden revealed just recently that he had heard the fae queen had only named the price of wedding a prince. She wanted you forced away from your kingdom, and there would be no remaining heirs. He says it was your father who managed a betrothal bargain with the prince of Rivenwilde so that you would have protection from the queen." At the mention of Lord Holden, Mireille had gestured to one of the men behind her, and at the mention of the prince, she'd casually gestured to him as if there was no difference in the men's stations. To the prince, she said, "It is true, is it not, that you might provide protection from a fae queen?"

The prince's brow lowered, but he said, "Any I name under my protection would be safe inside my home."

Mireille gave a single decisive nod as if the entire mystery was sewn up. Nickolas, however, had a thousand questions, not the least of which was what the fae prince gained by agreeing to harbor Jules. But Mireille had opened her mouth as if to speak again.

"All this to say," Gideon interrupted, "that if Jules renounces her title, she might marry a lord instead. The price would be paid, and the curse broken."

Jules went stock-still, like a statue among the grass in her pale muslin dress.

But Nickolas was moving again, chest bumping against the swords of two fae guards. *To marry one equal to my station*, she had said. Her price. If Gideon was right, Jules only needed a lord. It was all that stood between her and a broken curse. *Just one lord.* Nickolas heard himself say, "I am a lord."

Everyone turned to look at him.

"I am," he said defensively.

"Oh." Mireille's fingers twisted awkwardly at her waist. "I thought—well, I've brought along three of my best courtiers so that she might choose one of them and marry someone close to home."

Etta looked pained. Gideon was frowning. And Nickolas remembered, quite suddenly, that he was about to lose everything. He'd exposed the family's debt, his mother had been thrown into a cell, and Nickolas was a fae prisoner, only released on the condition that Jules wed the prince.

"Right," he said. "Of course. Best that she marries one of..." He glanced at the three men near Princess Mireille, all handsome, well-dressed, and evidently not at all put out by standing in a fae-filled forest or cowed by the prince. He swallowed thickly. "Don't know what I was thinking. Do carry on before it's too late."

"Can you do that?" Jules's voice was barely above a whisper, but it seemed to echo off the trees.

"He's the chancellor," Etta reminded her. "He can. And I can stand as witness. That makes two officials to seal the contract. It is all that is required."

"Renounce my title. Renounce my kingdom. Marry a lord."

Gideon drew one of the papers from the bundle tucked against the crook of his arm, the king's seal glinting in the torchlight. The chancery was guardian of the seal until a king was returned to office. Gideon truly did have the power to save her.

They could break her curse.

The prince clicked his tongue then said flatly, "Noal, seize the lady."

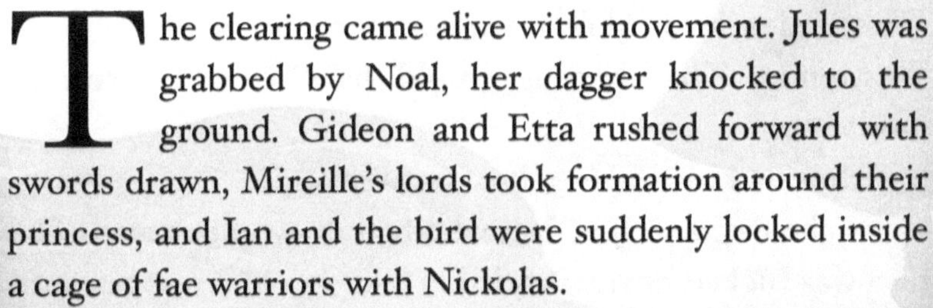

CHAPTER 19

The clearing came alive with movement. Jules was grabbed by Noal, her dagger knocked to the ground. Gideon and Etta rushed forward with swords drawn, Mireille's lords took formation around their princess, and Ian and the bird were suddenly locked inside a cage of fae warriors with Nickolas.

The prince lifted a hand, and Etta and Gideon seemed to slam into a wall of magic in their approach. They each fell a step backward, chests heaving, matching glares trained on the prince. Noal drew a fighting Jules closer to his chest, giving the prince room as he surveyed the crowd.

The prince said, "I was promised a bride, and a bride I shall have." He quirked a brow at Etta. "Unless you would like to war with Rivenwilde this night, Lady Ostwind."

The figures carved into the filigree wall seemed to move as if restless in anticipation. Vines curled outward from the wall, skirting the fae guards as they unfurled, reaching toward Jules and the prince. Noal kicked one of the vines away. The earth beneath Nickolas's feet felt alive with magic. In the shadowy trees, the fae creatures edged closer.

Etta lifted her sword as if she might rush the prince, but a marshal could not declare war—against the fae or anyone else. That responsibility would fall only to a general, and it was a keen reminder of previous battles between Westrende and the fae. Etta's jaw flexed. "If you take Jules through that wall, you will pay in ways you never imagined."

The prince's smile made clear he had every intention of doing so. "As she has said, she is not a citizen of Westrende. You have no claim on her, no call to intercede."

If she renounced her title and kingdom and married a Westrende lord, Jules would become a citizen of Westrende. The marshal would have every reason to intervene.

They had to get her out of Noal's hands.

Nickolas glanced at Ian, who had drawn his sword. The bird was tucked neatly inside his vest. Ian inclined his head infinitesimally, and Nickolas's fist tightened around the ring as he gave a small nod back. Together, they surged forward, Ian crashing low into the fae before them while Nickolas leapt through a narrow opening, gaining a cut to the arm and a mere few steps closer to the prince and Jules.

Fae magic surged through the ground, throwing another cage of roots between Nickolas and the prince. But Jules's ring was in his hand, and Nickolas burst through with a single slash of his sword. The prince's calm demeanor shifted to something decidedly more sinister, but Nickolas's step did not falter. An entire wall of roots and vines split the earth, exploding rich soil and greenery over Nickolas, but again, he slashed through with ease.

The prince shifted to face him before turning his palm open, and Noal quickly fumbled with a fighting Jules to hand over a finely made sword. The prince's long fingers curled around the hilt with practiced grace and something that spoke of his eagerness to engage.

"Nickolas, stop!" Gideon called from the sidelines as warnings and chatter rose from the watching crowd, trapped by fae magic.

"I'll renounce my citizenship," Nickolas said, his pace never slowing, attention never leaving the prince. "Do it, Gideon, before I drive my blade through this blackguard and be done with him once and for all."

The prince readied his stance. "Yes," he said. "Do it, Gideon."

Jules shouted, "No!" shoving hard into Noal then slamming a boot to his instep before driving an elbow up to connect with his chin. She lurched forward, half out of Noal's grip, just as Nickolas raised his sword and just as a cloud slid over the moon.

The sky went dark for one moment. In the next, a slow humming built, something beyond the trees drawing nearer. The breeze picked up again, the darkness cleared, and in the silvery light of the moon, five shapes came into view.

Nickolas's approach fell to a stop only paces away from the prince. Ian slammed into Nickolas from behind, jarring a curse out of Ian before his eyes, too, found the sky. They stared up with all the others as the shapes descended. The fae guards took a step back, Etta and Gideon several steps nearer. Mireille let out a sigh of what could only be delight.

Before anyone had even the inclination to throw her a quelling look, five giant birds dove into the clearing, the light glowing off their white wings. They did not slow to glide into a landing but came full force, whooping and grunting, knocking into the trellis, swooping at Noal's head, and crashing the altar to the ground. Two of them rammed into the prince, viciously pummeling until he dropped his sword. Evidently, the fae prince's magic was no match for a curse made by the queen, because he threw no root cages or walls of magic their way.

Jules came to her feet, eyes wet with evident joy. Her gaze met Ian's through the chaos, and in awe, Ian whispered, "They're here."

Had Ian not believed that Jules hadn't harmed her brothers, here was all the evidence he would need. The five elder brothers had returned in the form of birds, wreaking havoc just as Mireille had said.

"They're swans," Nickolas breathed.

Beside him, Frederick narrowed his birdy gaze.

Nickolas put up his hands. "It is neither here nor there. I only meant I was surprised."

Frederick's neck ruffled.

"We must hurry," Jules told the birds. "Time is nearly up."

Four of the birds circled the prince, while one drove its beak repeatedly at Noal until he stepped farther back. The fae guard remained on watch a careful distance away, swords at the ready.

"What's happening?" Nickolas whispered to Ian.

"No one acts against a fae queen" was all Ian said in return. But his eyes stayed on Jules, who had indeed acted against a fae queen's wishes.

Jules, who was about to overcome her curse.

Mireille and the three courtiers rushed forward with

Etta and Gideon, and Nickolas's throat went dry. There was a rush of introductions from Mireille, explanations about the contract from Etta and Gideon, and hurried arrangements. Nickolas opened his palm, staring down at the ring laced through the fine golden chain. He glanced up one last time at the prince, who stood watching the commotion with a resigned expression. It was done. Jules was safe. She would marry her lord.

Nickolas handed the ring to Ian then turned to go.

Behind him, the bickering abruptly cut off. "Lord Brigham," Jules called, the sound a bit jostled as if she was shoving through the crowd.

Nickolas stopped, unable to look at her lest she read the expression he was sure was plain on his face. The base of his hand was pressed to his breastbone, he realized, and he dropped it straightaway. "You're nearly out of time, my lady. Please, do not waste it on me."

She took hold of his elbow, tugging gently until he looked down at her. She was so close, her dark eyes shining up at him in the moonlight. Incomparable, that was what she was. And Nickolas did not know how to stop the *wanting* of her.

"Nickolas," she said softly. "You're still a lord."

The knife in his chest went deeper. Surely, there could be little left of the thing that had been his heart. "I'm not certain that's true any longer," he answered. "It's not worth the risk."

"If it was—"

"But it isn't. And you're out of time. Save yourself, my lady. Free your brothers. Please. I couldn't stand it if—I do not wish you to be unhappy."

She tugged him around to face her. "You are a lord,

Nickolas. Despite all the rest. Your debt has been answered. The records filed with chancery." At his expression, she explained, "I told you I would uphold my end of the bargain, and I have."

"You—" He swallowed hard. "What?"

"My kingdom is wealthy. *I* am wealthy. I could take none of it with me, but I ensured you and Frederick would be well taken care of, should I have ended up in the hands of the fae."

Nickolas's knees felt unsteady, but he had nowhere to sit. Jules's touch was all he had, and he clung to it with every fiber of his being. "You resolved my debt."

She nodded. "The Brighams are solvent. You remain a lord. I can do nothing to help free your mother, but perhaps that is for the best."

A helpless laugh bubbled up from his hollowed chest. "I am a lord."

"Yes," she said. "Now, would you—is it possible that you would be willing to—" She wet her lips. "Would you like to marry me, Lord Brigham?"

CHAPTER 20

Would you like to marry me? Jules had asked.

Nickolas stared down at her as she waited for an answer, disbelief overpowering his every instinct to shout, "Yes!" But it was no ploy. She was in earnest, and if he said yes, she could truly be his. And he would not be bringing her lower; he would be helping her escape a danger. Jules still had hold of Nickolas, and he slid his hand into hers, locking their thumbs, palms together, so that he might press her fingers to his lips after he carefully, calmly, not at all embarrassingly loudly shouted his *yes.*

He'd only opened his mouth to seal the bargain when Gideon's low voice broke in. "My lady, perhaps this isn't the best—"

Nickolas glared at Gideon before Jules turned to face the man. Etta, Mireille, and the three eligible lords stood at Gideon's back.

"What do you know of her best match?" Nickolas snapped. "Do you think her incapable of deciding that on her own?" He glanced at Jules. "Unless—if it's the coin you've settled upon me, my lady, that can be returned. I won't keep you from your own holdings."

Gideon frowned. "Of course it isn't that. She's never been concerned with a fortune, and even if she was, she might take her pick of the lords present to find ample wealth and stability."

"Stability?" Nickolas said. "So you think her incapable of choosing a husband who is stable. Dependable. Levelheaded."

Gideon gave him a look.

Jules stepped between the men. To Gideon, she said, "Lord Alexander, the paperwork is already drawn up, remember? Nickolas and I have both signed the marriage contract. It only needs sealed by your office."

He said, "I don't have time to go back for—"

Ian leaned in to hold a folded parchment he'd drawn from his vest in front of Gideon's face.

"I know you care about my well-being and only want what's best for me, Lord Alexander. But please, know that I go into this arrangement with a full understanding of what it means. Lord Brigham is my choice." She reached back to take Nickolas's hand. "Now, if you'd kindly proceed before the curse has ruined our last chance to save my brothers."

Repentant, Gideon inclined his head. He gestured for Nickolas and Jules to face forward and began an incredibly abridged version of the traditional recital, so swift that Nickolas had no time to panic that Jules might change her mind. Then Gideon asked, "Do each of you willingly enter into this agreement, aware that it is binding and may never be revoked?"

"I do," Jules said with such a lack of hesitation that

Nickolas forgot for a moment to breathe. She glanced up at him.

"I do," he said to only her.

"Very well." Gideon pressed the seal onto the contract, and the deed was done.

Frederick coughed up a feather. The dark bit of fluff and barbs flew into the gathering, startling Jules into taking a step backward and causing Ian to fumble the convulsing bird. At the center of the clearing, near the prince and his guard, the swans began to make calls of distress.

One of Jules's hands came up to cover her mouth, the other pressed to her midsection. The moon seemed to glow brighter, not a cloud in sight, and though there was no breeze, Nickolas felt a chill prickle his skin. He slid an arm around Jules's waist, terrified that the magic might somehow take her.

Frederick's body jerked once more, and Ian lowered him to the ground. There was a great deal of unpleasant cracking and popping sounds, but Jules never looked away, didn't bury her face in Nickolas's shoulder, and only watched in horror as she leaned against Nickolas for support. Then a full-sized leg clad in trousers shot from the body of the small gray bird, and everyone jumped a full step backward.

A second leg followed, then two arms, and the chest of the bird seemed to heave into a full set of ribs and shoulders beneath a fine embroidered tunic. Nickolas did not see when the head appeared, but he was grateful when the writhing finally stopped. Frederick—no longer a bird but a weedy young man with a kind, clean-shaven face and eyes very like his sister's—lay sprawled on the greensward, staring up at the sky. A long-fingered hand spread over his chest, adorned with a signet ring. He coughed once more, seemed momentarily on the edge of succumbing to emotion, then rolled onto his stomach before rising to his feet.

Ian reached out to steady him. Frederick appeared to find his balance then patted Ian's hand. His gaze rose to Jules. There was a moment of stillness before both began to weep. The next moment, Jules was in Frederick's arms. Mireille made a cooing sound. Then the group turned toward a commotion near the center of the clearing.

Five men of similar stature and build slapped one another on the arms, grabbing hold of tunics and exclaiming unintelligibly before making their way toward Frederick and Jules. She and Frederick broke through the crowd, rushing to meet their long-lost brothers. They picked Jules up in enthusiastic hugs, spinning her, mussed Frederick's dark hair, and traded embraces between rapid bouts of conversation.

Etta moved to Nickolas's side as they watched. A long breath eased out of her. "I'm glad you have found her."

A small helpless laugh escaped with his reply. "I had nothing to do with it. She found me."

He took in the scene and realized something did not quite sit right with him. Tone lowered, Nickolas asked, "Why is the prince still here?"

Expression grim, Etta did not respond. She remained at one side, sword in hand, as Gideon moved to Nickolas's other side.

"Etta?" Nickolas asked.

The others in the clearing appeared to become aware of the sense of unease, one by one turning toward the prince and his men. The six brothers surrounded Jules, none of them armed. The lords with Mireille resumed their swords.

The prince waited until they all gave him notice, a slow smile tipping up the edge of his lips. "Yes," he finally said. "All is well, the curse broken, and the happy family reunited." It seemed for a moment as if he might turn to go, but he stopped, holding up a single finger. "There remains but one final resolution. A tiny matter, really, of barely any consequence at all."

Nickolas's heart, overfull only moments before, felt on the edge of breaking all over. It was a fragile thing; he was not certain it could take losing Jules, not after all that had happened. He held his breath, waiting for the words to make sense but could not fathom what had been left unanswered. Jules was free, her curse broken. The prince could not want her for a wife, not with the marriage contract signed and sealed.

The prince's gaze connected with Jules's.

"What matter is that?" Jules asked coldly.

His answering grin revealed too many teeth. "Only the matter of an unsettled debt."

Etta and Gideon edged closer to Nickolas as the prince's guard raised their swords.

The prince flicked a glance at Etta before saying, "You all seem to have forgotten that Lord Brigham belongs to me."

CHAPTER 21

Nickolas felt the pronouncement like a blow to his midsection. The prince had planned it all along, had watched as Jules had chosen Nickolas and waited for their contract to be sealed.

The curse was broken, but he owned Jules's husband. Jules and the others moved nearer, surrounding Nickolas in an arc to face the fae guards and the prince. The prince strolled closer.

"You defaulted on our bargain, my lady. Until you pay that price, Lord Brigham will remain in Rivenwilde with me."

Jules reached around her back and pulled a second thin blade from somewhere within her simple dress.

"No!" Gideon and Nickolas called. Gideon, perhaps, because Jules was now a citizen of Westrende and could not harm the Rivenwilde prince per an ancient dictate but Nickolas because he did not want her to be hurt.

The prince reached forward, and Nickolas was pulled across the greensward, half the distance to the prince.

Nickolas fumbled for the ring then remembered he'd given it to Ian. Besides, the curse was broken. Whatever magic it held was likely gone. Which meant he and Jules—and the entire crowd of onlookers—had no protection from fae magic.

Boots hovering just above the tall grass, Nickolas was powerless to do anything at all. "It's all right," he told Jules. "You're safe. You're free. That's what matters." It would be tolerable if he could be certain of at least that much. Whatever the prince did, Nickolas could withstand it, knowing the torment was paid to him instead of Jules.

Jules's lips parted, her eyes glinting in the strange play of moon and torchlight. "I cannot—" she started, but Etta stepped forward.

"Those are your terms, then?" Etta's grip flexed on her sword hilt, making no secret of her desire to drive the villain through. "A princess in exchange for Lord Brigham's release?"

The prince chuckled. "Yes. Only that. A princess for Rivenwilde and you may have your Lord Brigham back."

"Done," Etta said. She snapped a signal, and Gideon came forward.

The prince's brows drew together, seeming more annoyed than confused, and he said, "Jules is married and a mere lady. She does me no good. A titled princess is the price, nothing less."

"Yes," Etta said. "We heard. Gideon has the paperwork here. The princess is yours. Lord Brigham is ours. Release him."

"Lady Ostwind," the prince started, plainly irritated, but his words fell off as Mireille leaned around Etta to give the prince a friendly little wave.

"Mireille?" Jules said. "You can't throw her to the—"

Etta hushed Jules with both a reprimanding hiss and gesture.

Jules straightened as if prepared to argue further, but Mireille stepped past them both to face the prince. "It's me," she said. "Princess Mireille of Norcliffe. I'm certain you know of my family. Most people do." She smiled conspiratorially. "I come to you willingly. Though, if you're agreeable to a small delay, I wouldn't mind a few days to get my affairs in order before I go. The chancellor was kind enough to draw up a contract, guaranteeing my return so that Nickolas may be released without delay—" She glanced at Nickolas, who by now surely looked as pained as he felt, dangling by magic above the clearing. "I would consider it a great favor to me should you let him down. Not that you owe any favors to me, only that it would be so very unkind to keep him from Jules even a heartbeat longer after all she's been through. The poor thing."

The prince blinked.

Gideon crossed the distance to hand him a piece of fine parchment, presumably the aforementioned guarantee, and the prince glanced at it with what could only be aggrieved bewilderment.

"It's all legal," Etta said. "By both your law and ours."

"So, you assume I'll just—" The prince's words cut off when Noal cleared his throat. The prince did not even look at the man. "Yes. Very well." He shoved the contract back at Gideon. "I do not need your paper. I am the prince of the Riven Court."

He flicked a hand, and Nickolas's boots crashed to the earth. "Lord Brigham is free." His lip curled as Jules rushed to Nickolas's side, then his gaze rolled over the six brothers, the three lords, and Ian, Gideon, and Etta. "It would bring me great pleasure should I never see any of you again." Shoulders square, he adjusted his jacket, drew up his chin, and met Mireille's gaze.

He tipped forward in a small bow. When he rose again, he said, "Shall you neglect to call for me, know that I intend to come to collect."

Mireille smiled in that way that shifted her right eye, not so unlike a wink. The prince regarded her for a moment then turned and walked toward the wall. Noal did not acknowledge the crowd before following, then every fae guard disappeared through the ancient wall behind them.

"Well," Mireille said. "It looks like I'll have that adventure after all."

Nickolas and Jules stared at her.

"Come," Etta told them. "We can discuss this all once we're safely outside the forest."

The chittering creatures that had restlessly observed the goings-on paced more eagerly in the spaces between the trees. Gideon handled Nickolas the sword that had been knocked from him when the prince's magic had taken hold then glanced at the six brothers, likely wishing they had weapons of their own.

Jules's hand slid into Nickolas's, palm against palm, and the entire group marched forward through the woods.

IT WAS the small hours before dawn when the group had finally resumed the safety of the castle. Princess Mireille and her men had returned to their suites, Ian was being tended for a minor cut he'd received in their scuffle with the fae guard, and Nickolas and Jules sat nestled between Jules's brothers as Etta and Gideon distributed hot tea and what honey cakes and bread they could find. Jules had not let go of Nickolas's hand.

The moment Etta finally settled—not onto a chair but leaned against a desk across from Nickolas and Jules—she asked, "What can you tell us of Rivenwilde?"

The cake seemed to catch in Nickolas's throat.

Etta crossed her arms. "As I suspected, you are bound from revealing a single of the prince's secrets under the laws of hospitality."

The statement came in such a way that Nickolas guessed it was not the first time the prince had foiled her attempts at information gathering, but the expression on Etta's face made clear it was not the time to question her about it.

"What about Mireille?" Jules asked. "You cannot be planning to actually let her go."

Etta tapped a finger against the sleeve of her marshal's coat. Jules had intended to do just such a thing but evidently could not countenance it for someone else. Etta said, "Mireille offered herself in exchange for Nickolas because she needs protection from a threat much greater than the prince." When Jules started to speak again, Etta held up a hand. "I am not to say more on the matter. But trust that it was done willingly and with utmost consideration."

Jules's mouth snapped shut.

One of the brothers slid a hand over hers. "The fae queen causes a great deal of strife, sister. You have been gone for so long and I fear do not understand the full reach of her influence." His expression was apologetic. "Despite all our efforts, she has managed to corrupt our father past the point of return."

"Is he well?"

Another of the brothers answered, "Not entirely. And worse, he's in grave danger from the queen, and that danger puts the kingdom at risk."

The tea turned in Nickolas's stomach. Jules had said that if she agreed to wed the prince, she would be putting entire kingdoms in danger. And there was her brother, free of his curse, echoing the sentiment once more. Nickolas had no notion of what a fae queen might be capable of, but their tones made clear it was worse than the threat of the Rivenwilde prince.

"The queen is going to marry him," Jules breathed.

The first brother inclined his head. "A date has been set. And once he does... Well, I'm certain we all know her plans for Father."

Jules's hand tightened in Nickolas's as her brother drew away. She asked, "How do we stop it?"

The second brother leaned forward. "We must remove him from the throne before the ceremony is complete."

"I support your decision," she said. "Even though, as I've renounced both title and kingdom, you no longer need my consent."

The brothers glanced at one another.

"What is it?" Jules asked warily.

The one who appeared oldest drew back his shoulders, giving Jules his full attention. It was quite impressive, Nickolas noticed, but Jules did not seem in the least cowed.

The man said, "We have decided to step down. It is not we who deserve this honor. You have broken our curse, defied the fae queen, and sacrificed all in order to preserve the kingdom."

"That's—I can't. I'm no longer even—"

The lot of them stood, moved to face Jules, then knelt on the floor before her as one, heads bowed.

A hush fell over the room before the eldest lifted his gaze to hers. "Julietta Leanna Eleanora Declare, I hereby bestow upon you the right of heir, as my sister, daughter of the king, and honorable servant to the kingdom. Long may you reign."

"Hear, hear," echoed the brothers. "Long may you reign."

"I—" Jules's words seemed to choke off, her hand gone slack in Nickolas's.

For Nickolas's part, he was certain he'd gone at least as pale as Gideon and Etta had. He could not help but ask them, "Why are you looking at me like that?"

Etta opened her mouth, but no words came. Gideon ran a shaky hand across his brow.

"There is no choice," one of the brothers said. "If we do not remove the king now, he will certainly be killed as soon as they're wed."

"And the fae queen will sit upon the throne," said another.

"But—" Jules began.

The oldest stood, reaching forward to place a gentle hand on her shoulder. "We have been touched by the queen's magic, sister. You have not. You are the best hope for this kingdom. Your heart is honest, just, and true, and we have faith in you above all others. Trust that we have not made this decision lightly."

Jules swallowed. "Then I will do my best. You have my word."

The others stood, their mood resolved and decidedly more hopeful.

Nickolas felt as if he'd just stepped off a swaying ship. "I—so this means you'll be queen."

Jules's gaze snapped to his, her brows drawn together. "It does."

He drew a shallow breath, unable to tolerate more, and gave a small nod. "When do you leave?"

"Nickolas, you mustn't—are you saying you won't come with me?"

Nickolas did not know what he was saying, only that it hurt very much to speak, and he felt a bit light-headed. He rubbed a palm over his chest. It must have been the cakes. Honey cakes had never agreed with him.

"You will come, won't you?" Jules asked.

"I—do you want me to come?"

"Of course." She let out a shaky breath. "It is not as if I could do this without you."

"Of course," he repeated. He'd no deuced idea what she meant by not being able to do it without him, but he wasn't about to disagree with her. Wherever it was, whatever she needed, he would be there.

Gideon released a low oath then whispered, "Do we tell him?" before Etta replied just as quietly, "Best let him work it out on his own."

"It's been a very long day," Jules told the room. "Perhaps we should discuss the rest tomorrow." She gave a gentle squeeze to Nickolas's hand. "Lord Brigham, won't you walk with me in the courtyard?"

"Of course," he said again. They stood, then he turned once more to Etta. "What's to happen to my mother?"

Etta rose from her position on the desk. "She will remain a prisoner until the council makes their judgment. If you would like, you may offer a statement in her defense before the trial."

Nickolas nodded. He understood well enough what the council's judgment would be. Lady Brigham would receive no leniency when it was revealed that she'd both committed a crime and made a bargain with the fae, no matter what Nickolas had to say on the matter. "Then, I will have guardianship of my sisters, it seems."

Jules slid her hand through his arm. "They'll be no bother at all. We can find a lovely place for them. Did I tell you, Lord Brigham, of the courtyard gardens I played in as a girl? The most beautiful roses and violets grow there, right around a fishpond stocked with trout. Do you fish? I'm afraid I've never asked you."

He stared down at her as she spoke, aware that he was being drawn from the chancery office and through the unlit corridor, but Nickolas could not make himself care. Not when Jules's arm was locked with his, the pair of them finally safe from harm.

They walked through several corridors before Jules drew him into a lesser-used passage that came out nowhere near where he might have expected. His steps slowed, and she slowed with him.

He said, "This is Carvell's wing."

"As a matter of fact, the Carvells have gone away for a bit." She tugged him back to her. "The marshal's office discovered the family had ties to a crime. Something about forgery and extortion."

"Extortion," Nickolas repeated.

Jules hummed in affirmation. "I believe Lord Keller has already inquired about purchasing the grounds. He plans to install several water features in the courtyard."

A choked laugh came from Nickolas just as they neared the arched doorway outside said courtyard.

Jules reached for the lever, meeting his gaze. "I thought it might be nice to visit once more. This time, without interruptions."

His heart woke again, swelling to the walls of his chest, and when he took a lungful of the cool predawn air, Nickolas felt more like himself. But that was not right, because it was a version of himself that was free from the burdens of debts, secrets, and the sense that time was running out. Nickolas was alone with Jules in a lovely garden, and he did not have a single other place he wanted to be.

She kept hold of his hand, drawing him with her over the stone pathway, through violets and poppies and the statuary he had forgotten was nearly all nude. At a bare spot of grass, she stopped and asked for his jacket. He removed it and spread it over the ground, and the pair of them settled, backs to the low edge wall, to stare up at the stars.

Jules nestled closer, her body warm beneath his arm, and he turned his face toward her as she watched the night sky. "My lady," he said quietly. "Now that you are my wife..."

Her head tilted nearer as if to better hear, though the courtyard was silent.

Nickolas let his voice dip even lower. "Does that mean I can kiss you?"

The curve of her cheek shifted with her smile as she

answered, "I'm afraid it means you must. As often as possible. And you should call me Jules."

He leaned in, his lips only a breath from her bare neck when he said, "Jules." She shivered, but when his mouth touched her skin, Jules melted against him. His lips trailed slowly up to her jaw, brushing the sensitive flesh beneath her ear before Nickolas pulled back just enough to let her turn to him. The light in her eyes was playful and content as she came forward to meet him in a kiss. It was soft and sweet, unrushed because there was nothing but this for as long as forever.

"Or at least until tomorrow," Jules murmured.

Nickolas could barely murmur the "What?" that slipped between the brush of their lips, lost again to the unbearable contentment of the moment.

"Nothing," she said. "Never mind."

"Saints," he breathed. "We should have been doing this the entire time we were engaged."

"No idea what you were waiting for," she said as her fist balled into the material of his shirt to drag him back. "Must make up for lost time. Only thing for it."

He slid a thumb against her cheek, fingers at the base of her neck tipping her head toward his. "Noted."

THE ORANGE PINK of sunrise lit the sky when Nickolas's awareness surfaced again. He wasn't certain if he'd dozed off, only that his limbs felt liquid and his eyes heavy. If Jules had meant to watch the sunrise, she'd missed it. Laid against him, her legs sprawled beneath the long skirt, boots canted in opposite directions. She looked impossibly peaceful. One arm was wrapped firmly around him, the other tucked beneath her, hand tangled in the material of his jacket. Her hair had fallen from its pins, long locks of it soft against his skin.

He had the thought that he should wake her but could not quite bring himself to disturb such needed rest. It was followed by the thought that he could carry her, take her back to her rooms where she could stretch comfortably in her own bed.

Then, with a jolt, Nickolas recalled that she was his wife. Her rooms would in fact, be not in the chancery, but his own suite. That was when Nickolas, Lord Brigham, remembered that Jules was a queen. That a queen's husband was...

"Saints," he wheezed. "That's not—"

Jules shifted, snuggling closer to wrap both arms around his waist. Nickolas's words dried up. He could not bear to wake her, only smoothed his hand over her shoulder as he forced himself to relax once more against the wall. He would have to come to terms with what had happened but that was a worry for outside their courtyard garden. There, he was with Jules, and the world was silent, and with her in his arms, he eventually drifted off to sleep.

Weeks later, Nickolas stood atop the small knoll overlooking the impossibly grand garden on the palace lawn of the warm and sunny kingdom in which his wife had been named queen. He tried not to think on it too much, because it still hurt his head. Jules's brothers granting the throne to their younger sister had not only illustrated to the kingdom their full support but that she was without fault in her father's dealings with the fae.

The fae queen had been ousted once those bound to her by bargain or loyalty had been removed and any claim on their father or the throne was resolved. No one was certain where she had gone, only that she had given up her ploy far more easily than anticipated. Jules's father had suffered greatly at the hands of the fae queen but seemed more restful once she was gone and his heirs returned.

For her part, Jules had shined. She possessed a calm authority and wielded her easy ability to disregard or focus on the chattering of others like a weapon. Maneuvering courtiers did not stand a chance.

She glanced up at Nickolas from where she stood at his side in a simple gown of the richest fabrics, a thin gold crown woven into her upswept hair. "Will you always look at me in such a manner, or do you suppose it will wear off in time?"

He grinned. "I cannot seem to help it. You are too lovely to look away from, you make me unbearably happy, and, I'm afraid, indecently proud to call you my wife."

On Jules's other side, Frederick rolled his eyes. "One can only hope it wears off soon. I can't fathom what a man would do with more pride than you."

"Someday," Nickolas murmured as his gaze trailed over Jules's skin, "you will find something that satisfies you half as much as this life does me. And that day, you will have to eat your crotchety words."

Frederick scoffed.

The smile in Jules's gaze was only for Nickolas. Then she returned to watching the lawn, where the other five of her brothers idled among the flowers with Nickolas's sisters, Ian, and several members of court. "It seems we've a great many such pairings to look forward to. I can only hope that whomever each of our loved ones find are as well matched."

Nickolas managed to tear his gaze away to take in his sisters, their bare golden locks standing out among a sea of dark top hats and ribboned bonnets. The eldest was speaking closely to one of Jules's brothers. He could not object to her finding a prince, but he did not think he could wish any of his sisters on souls so kind as the

Declares. Well, maybe Frederick. But that was where he drew the line.

His youngest sister knelt before a tame rabbit, and Nickolas edged closer to Jules. "Did you say you were once given a menagerie?" His gaze connected with hers once more. "What precisely did you let out of that cage as a girl?"

Jules's lip twitched. "Lions. Among other things."

Nickolas barked a startled laugh, earning a glance from the courtiers who'd engaged Frederick in conversation. "Truly, the heart of a warrior. I am delighted to call you my queen."

She turned to face him, shutting out the entire courtyard with just that bit of attention. "You mustn't," she reminded him. "I am their queen. To you, I am only—"

He leaned in, voice low as he took her hand in his. "It is not as if I could ever forget, love." He lifted their hands to brush a soft kiss over Jules's knuckles. "Your name is etched on the walls of my heart."

Discover more in the Rivenwilde world with the prince's story (and Mireille!), *Upon the Riven Throne*

Rivenwilde Series

iREENCHAU

Bound by Prophecy

Shifting Fate

Reign of Shadows

SHATTERED REALMS

King of Ash and Bone

Queen of Iron and Blood

- **WITCHY PNR** -

HAVENWOOD FALLS

Toil and Trouble

BAD MEDICINE

Blood & Brute & Ginger Root

Visit the author on the web at

www.melissa-wright.com

www.ingramcontent.com/pod-product-compliance
Lightning Source LLC
Chambersburg PA
CBHW030848200726
48285CB00007B/2608